You met Adam St. Clair in *Return to Yesterday*. In *Adam's Story*, read more about him and the woman who saves his life...and teaches him about love.

"I Enjoy Being Alone."

"You feel safer being alone, you mean. There's a difference." Adam reached down and gently pulled her up to stand in front of him.

Cupping his hands around her face, he tilted her head so that she was looking up at him from only a few inches away. "You've left out one very important ingredient in your life, you know."

Her eyes felt locked to his gaze. She could feel his body aligned against hers and could barely prevent the shiver that tingled down her spine.

"What's that?" Caitlin managed to ask.

"You've allowed no room in your life for love." Adam closed the distance between them, pulling her closer against him while he did what he'd been wanting to do for days...weeks...possibly a lifetime.

He kissed her.

Dear Reader:

Series and Spin-offs! Connecting characters and intriguing interconnections to make your head whirl.

In Joan Hohl's successful trilogy for Silhouette Desire—*Texas Gold* (7/86), *California Copper* (10/86), *Nevada Silver* (1/87)—Joan created a cast of characters that just wouldn't quit. You figure out how *Lady Ice* (5/87) connects. And in August, "J.B." demanded his own story—*One Tough Hombre*. In *Falcon's Flight*, coming in November, you'll learn *all* about...?

Annette Broadrick's *Return to Yesterday* (6/87) introduced Adam St. Clair. This August *Adam's Story* tells about the woman who saves his life—and teaches him a thing or two about love!

The six Branigan brothers appeared in Leslie Davis Guccione's *Bittersweet Harvest* (10/86) and *Still Waters* (5/87). September brings *Something in Common*, where the eldest of the strapping Irishmen finds love in unexpected places.

Midnight Rambler by Linda Barlow is in October—a special Halloween surprise, and totally unconnected to anything.

Keep an eye out for other Silhouette Desire favorites—Diana Palmer, Dixie Browning, Ann Major and Elizabeth Lowell, to name a few. You never know when secondary characters will insist on their own story....

All the best,

Isabel Swift
Senior Editor & Editorial Coordinator
Silhouette Books

ANNETTE BROADRICK
Adam's Story

Silhouette Desire

Published by Silhouette Books New York

America's Publisher of Contemporary Romance

SILHOUETTE BOOKS
300 East 42nd St., New York, N.Y. 10017

Copyright © 1987 by Annette Broadrick

ISBN: 0-373-05367-3

First Silhouette Books printing August 1987

America's Publisher of Contemporary Romance

Printed in the U.S.A.

ANNETTE BROADRICK

lives on the shores of the Lake of the Ozarks in Missouri, where she spends her time doing what she loves most—reading and writing romantic fiction. "For twenty-five years I lived in various large cities, working as a legal secretary, a very high-stress occupation. I never thought I was capable of making a career change at this point in my life, but thanks to Silhouette I am now able to write full-time in the peaceful surroundings that have turned my life into a dream come true."

This book is dedicated to those people—and you know who you are—who helped me to understand psychic abilities and how they work....
My grateful appreciation.

One

Adam St. Clair paused for a moment outside his luxury hotel and looked up and down the Monterrey, Mexico, thoroughfare. The February wind off the mountains caused him to raise the collar of his sheepskin-lined denim jacket and to settle his Stetson more firmly on his head.

Hunching his shoulders against the wind, Adam started toward his car.

Tonight was the night. He wasn't sure how he knew, exactly. He'd lost count of the number of leads he'd followed since he'd joined the agency that was trying to stop the flood of drugs crossing the border between Mexico and the United States. Most of them had led nowhere. Some had gotten him into the circle of men who made their living bringing drugs in from South America.

He'd had no trouble with his cover. Playing the part of a Texas rancher came naturally to him—that's who he was, what he'd always been. Then two years ago he'd become something more—a man determined to do what he could to stop what was happening in his country.

If all went well tonight, he'd have the information necessary to stop one of the major leaders, unless his informant changed his mind.

It was up to Adam to make sure the man didn't change his mind.

He sat in his car for a few minutes, waiting for the heater to warm the chilled interior. According to the directions given to him, he had several hours of hard driving to do, back into the remote area of the mountains.

Adam had removed his hat when he got into the car. Now he ran his hand through his tawny hair, causing the waves to fall into curls across his forehead. His sister, Felicia, had always enjoyed teasing him about his curls. His mouth lifted into a slight smile at the memory. His sister had been able to get away with a great deal. He loved her very much.

Reaching for the ignition switch Adam forced his thoughts back to the job at hand. He knew that what he was doing was dangerous, had always known that. He felt a twinge of guilt that he'd never told Felicia about this part of his life. But it was better this way. There was no reason for her to be involved, and since she'd been living in Los Angeles for the past several years, he'd had no need to make explanations to anyone about his periodic trips to Mexico.

He glanced at his watch. It was time to go. He hoped this wasn't another one of those fruitless contacts where nobody showed up.

Adam pulled away from his parking space and followed the streets until they connected with the highway that led out of town. Another long evening had begun.

Her eyes flew open, and Caitlin Moran sat up in bed. She looked around her small one-room mountain cabin, trying to decide what had awakened her. Glancing at the windows, she noted that the darkness outside showed no sign of impending dawn.

Caitlin continued to sit there, listening intently. Something was wrong. She slid out of bed, absently pulled on her heavy robe to offset the February chill of the mountains and padded to the window silently.

She could see nothing in the clearing except the heavy frost that tinted the blades of grass silver. Nothing moved. Listening, she could hear the rustling sounds from the surrounding mountainside as the nocturnal birds and animals went about the serious occupation of surviving in the wilderness. She could hear no sound of an intruder.

Then why had she awakened so abruptly? Because of the long hours she put in and the strenuous exercise due to the primitive life-style she led, Caitlin never had to worry about falling asleep at night. And morning arrived so quickly each day, bringing with it a myriad of occupations to keep her busy, that she rarely, if ever, woke before dawn.

Disturbed, but unsure why, Caitlin turned away from the window and walked over to the stone fireplace that covered the north wall of the cabin. Coals still glowed brightly through the ashes. She added more wood and watched while hungry tongues of flame suddenly licked the new additions, causing them to smolder, then to glow.

Caitlin stood there for a moment, staring into the flames and warming her hands, filled with unease.

What could be wrong?

She received no answers. Reluctantly turning away from the fire, she crawled back into bed, pulling the blankets around her neck.

Caitlin wasn't alarmed because she was alone. She had lived in her small cabin, high in the mountains near Monterrey, Mexico, for more than five years. Being alone was a way of life for her, one she had chosen.

Staring up at the roof over her head, acknowledging the sturdiness that had sheltered her so well, she tried to calm her mind, letting it drift as it would, willing herself to fall asleep again.

Instead, scenes began to race across the screen of her mind—scenes of violence and destruction. She saw two cars traveling fast over twisting and narrow mountain roads, their blinding headlights bathing the surrounding countryside with an eerie glow.

A shadowed face appeared. At first the features of the face were indistinct, but with practiced concentration Caitlin began to see more of the details as they focused into clear, clean lines. Gray-green eyes with a look of determination and agitation stared back at her, a frown causing the brows to draw together over a well-formed nose. A strong jawline appeared to be clenched, the lines around the tight-lipped mouth making deep grooves in the face.

Caitlin knew she had never seen the man before. She also knew that she would never forget him.

Who was he? She shook her head in frustration. Although his skin appeared to be deeply tanned, she knew he was not a native of Mexico. Tawny curls fell across his forehead, giving a deceptively boyish look to an otherwise stern countenance.

Who was he? She tried to get more, but nothing came. She sighed, frustrated with her ability to see so much that she didn't want to see, and her inability to pick up more when she tried.

She had lived with her frustration long enough to know there was little she could do to rid her mind of the pictures and messages she received. She had tried. Desperately. Caitlin wanted nothing more than to be the normal young woman who had planned her life so carefully all those years ago.

Being brought up by two people who loved her and each other with a warm, generous love had ill-prepared her for the traumatic events that had torn her life apart, leaving her like some sort of freak.

She forced herself to turn over, trying to blank her mind of all thoughts. Instead she began to remember how she had slowly made a place for herself here in the mountains. She couldn't recall how long she had lived here alone before she made friends with the local people.

About once a month she would take the vegetables she had grown and the hand-woven rugs and material down to the small settlement a few miles from her cabin. There she would trade for the supplies she needed.

The people of the village would stare at her reddish-gold hair and blue eyes with suspicion and distrust. Why was she living there? What did she want?

How could she explain to them that she was searching for some answers? She was looking for her sanity, her belief in herself, her ability to function in a world that no longer made any sense to her.

How could she explain what she didn't truly understand herself? All she knew was that by the time she'd finally been released from the hospital, she'd known her life would never be the same again. Her loving parents were gone. The friendships she trusted in and counted on had evaporated, and the man she loved had withdrawn from her in suspicion and distaste.

The stoic natives would probably not be impressed to know that she had run from the world and had chosen their small corner of the universe to find shelter and some measure of peace.

Caitlin had been grateful for the many summers she had spent with her aunt in San Antonio. Languages had come easily to her, and Spanish had a lilting, rollicking cadence that she had enjoyed learning, so that by the time she returned to Seattle each fall, she had continued to increase her vocabulary and her grasp of the language.

Her parents had been amused and had encouraged her to take the language in school, as well. At the time she'd had no thought of adopting Spanish as her own language. Now she couldn't remember the last time she'd spoken English. Probably not since her aunt had passed away.

Caitlin had lost all ties with the woman she'd been before she moved to the mountains. She preferred her life now and rarely thought of the past.

She'd grown used to the villagers and had learned not to expect anyone but the shopkeepers to speak to her. She understood and identified with the villagers' need for privacy. They didn't bother her, and she didn't bother them.

She remembered the day she had been on her way out of the village, leading her burro—who carried a month's worth of supplies for her—when she heard a baby crying. When she paused, she realized there was no baby crying around her, yet she heard the choked whimpering very clearly in her head. Rubbing her forehead with frustration, Caitlin almost groaned aloud.

Since she had moved to the mountains, the pictures and impressions she kept seeing had slowly disappeared, finally leaving her free from their insistent pressure.

Now they were back, and she wasn't sure what to do. The choked crying of the baby indicated that it was sick. The health of the infant was none of her business, but she had a sense that she could help him. Did she dare offer? Would the parents accept her help?

There was only one way to find out.

The sounds of the crying baby seemed to fill her mind once more, and Caitlin made her decision. She began to thread her way through the streets in an effort to locate the infant, walking around dogs and chickens, skirting pigpens, while the sound increasingly grew in her mind.

When she paused in front of a small house, she realized there was no actual sound coming from within. Yet she felt certain the baby was inside. She could see in her mind's eye the baby being held in its mother's arms.

With a great deal of uncertainty and trepidation, Caitlin tapped on the door. After a long moment the door slowly opened, and a young woman with tired, reddened eyes peered out at her. Groping for her best Spanish, Caitlin said, "Your baby is ill?"

"Oh, yes! I fear he is dying!" was the distressed reply.

"May I help?"

"How can you help?" was the agonized response.

Caitlin reached into her cloth bag and pulled out a smaller one. "I have had some experience in healing with these herbs. May I see your child?"

Later Caitlin realized that the only reason the young mother allowed her to come in was because she had already given up hope. When Caitlin stepped into the dimly lit room, she saw the other women, sitting in a circle around the infant, weeping.

The poor infant struggled for every breath. He seemed incapable of crying at this point. Caitlin asked for boiling water, and as soon as it was brought to her, she crushed some leaves into it and quickly made a tent with a blanket lying nearby. She picked up the baby and held him, sitting under the blanket and breathing with him, absorbing the aromatic fumes that enveloped them both.

Then she began to croon to him, rubbing her hands over his body and talking to him in a low voice, explaining there was nothing to fear, that breathing was easy, part of life, that there was nothing to fear from life, that he would enjoy it.

Caitlin continued to request that hot water be added, and she continued to hold the baby upright, forcing his lungs to expel the fluids that were strangling him. And when he began to cough, she helped him rid himself of the life-threatening substance.

Time meant nothing to her as she worked with the baby. Slowly his breathing eased, and his temperature lowered. His color improved, and after several hours he dropped off into a deep, healing sleep.

When Caitlin stood up to place him in his bed, she realized she was stiff from sitting in one position for so long, holding the baby.

She turned and looked at the mother with a smile. "What is your baby's name?"

"Miguel."

Caitlin gently stroked the infant's back while she spoke to the mother.

"I believe that Miguel will be all right now. When he awakens, make him a liquid from soaking these leaves in boiling water for five minutes. Give him this much," she showed the woman a measurement, "every two hours. By tomorrow he will be ready to eat again."

A clamoring of voices broke out from all the women, and Caitlin was too tired to decipher what they were saying, but it didn't matter. Their actions clearly spelled out that they were elated with her success.

She began to back out of the room, saying over and over, *"De nada, de nada."*

The women followed her into the street, touching her hair lightly, clearly enthralled with what she had done.

Now that the crisis was over, Caitlin discovered that her energy had drained out of her like sand quickly running out of a bag. She had to get home. Smiling and nodding to the women, Caitlin waved her appreciation for their thanks and led her burro away.

The next day Antonio, Miguel's father, appeared at her door, together with his father and two brothers, asking what they could do to pay her for saving the young child's life. She tried to explain they owed her nothing, but they insisted. When they saw how simply she was living there, they told her they would bring her new furniture to replace the small cot she slept on and the crating box she used for a table.

And they had. Over the months each one had shown up at her doorstep with a new offering—a beautifully carved bed, a small round table with four matching chairs, a rocker.

They had brought to her their greatest gifts—their love—and she felt abundantly blessed.

Eventually the surrounding mountainside heard the story of the fair-haired healer who knew mysterious ways to use the plants of the fields and forests to bring strength and peace to a troubled body and soul. She spent many of her days, when she wasn't working in her garden or making hand-spun garments on her loom, traveling from one isolated mountain home to another—visiting, listening, and at times, offering a healing, whether it was of the body, of the mind, or of the spirit.

Caitlin felt truly blessed to have found what she could do with her life. And she was content....

She was almost asleep, lulled by her thoughts of the life she had established here in the mountains, when suddenly, once again, an image of the same face leaped into her mind, a look of dread and horror engulfing its taut expression.

Caitlin involuntarily screamed, "No!"

She shook with the intensity of the feeling that gripped her. The man was in danger, and she needed to help him. But where was he? And where was the danger?

Throwing back the covers, she leaped up and pulled on jeans and a soft woven shirt that tied at the neck. She felt around for the heavy boots she wore when hiking and, finding them, quickly pulled them on over thick socks.

Grabbing her heavy hooded coat and the bag that she always carried, Caitlin threw open the door of the cabin and stepped outside.

The stillness of the night wrapped itself around her in a harmonious serenity that temporarily soothed her. *All is well,* it seemed to say to her.

But she knew better. A man was near death, and she needed to find him. She didn't know where he was or how he had been hurt, but she knew she had to find him.

The crude shelter that protected Arturo, her burro, lay several yards from her front door, and she hastened toward the stall where Arturo slept. She found his bridle and blanket, but instead of attempting to ride, she grabbed his halter and led him away from the warmth of his home, much to his loudly voiced irritation.

"Oh, hush, Arturo," she scolded impatiently. "It won't be long until dawn, anyway. So we're getting an early start on the day. There's no reason to make a scene about it." She scratched behind his ear and he turned his head and looked at her.

She laughed. "All right. So you'll get extra oats tonight; is that a deal? You're already too fat, you know. The exercise will be good for you."

Caitlin hurried down the path, leading the recalcitrant animal and trying to get her bearings.

A desperate sense of urgency pushed her on, but she couldn't pinpoint where it was leading her. She was moving away from the village, even farther away from civilization than her own home, which was isolated. Where was she going? And why?

Wherever it was, she needed to travel quickly, and she continually urged Arturo to hurry, tugging at his halter and promising him all sorts of treats once they returned home.

The path narrowed to no more than a trail where deer and other animals followed the mountain ridge over into the next valley.

Caitlin had never been here before. As far as she knew, no one lived in these parts, particularly not anyone who looked like the man she had seen.

Coming over a ridge, she saw a light moving in the distance. She paused, watching the headlights of two cars.

One vehicle seemed to be chasing the other through the mountain stillness, following twisting, turning roads. She remembered seeing them earlier in her mind. Tired of tugging the lazy burro, she quickly tied him to a young sapling and hurried toward the lights.

She watched with mounting horror while one of the cars began to ram the back of the other car, making the driver lose control. The car in the lead careened back and forth, then grazed a tree, causing the car to roll as though in slow motion, coming to rest at the edge of the steep precipice.

From her position high up on the mountain, Caitlin watched in horror as the scene continued to unfold before her. All the details seemed to have taken place in slow motion, the sound of the squealing brakes and crumpling metal loud in the silence of the night. She broke into a run, then came to an abrupt halt when two men leaped out of the vehicle that had given chase and ran to the other car. She could hear them clearly, their voices carrying in the night.

"Where is he? Is he dead?" one asked in Spanish.

"I don't know. Is he in the car?" The other started toward the car that was leaning drunkenly over the side.

"No. Wait! Here he is. He was thrown out."

She saw a flash, as though from a camera.

"Is he dead?"

"If not, he will be soon enough. Let's get that car over the side. If anyone finds him, they'll think he was just driving too fast and lost control."

Caitlin could hardly believe what she was hearing. These men had done everything they could to cause the other car to wreck. Now they intended to abandon the injured man.

She continued her way down the mountainside, a sense of helplessness overwhelming her. Not only was she outnumbered, she had a hunch those two wouldn't hesitate to kill her if they knew she'd been a witness to what they had done. She watched as the men pushed on the car until it toppled over the side and exploded on impact.

The noise shook the ground, and Caitlin grabbed the limb of a nearby tree to keep her balance.

She heard one of them say "Let's roll him over the side," just as Arturo protested the noise, the night, and being left alone. Caitlin froze, wondering if the men would investigate the sound.

One of them glanced up in her direction.

"What was that?"

"Who knows? There's all kinds of animals living out here."

The other man headed back to the car. "Let's go. Nobody's going to find him here, anyway."

Caitlin saw the first man bend over the motionless form that was spotlighted by the beams of the car. After a moment, he stood up and shrugged. "No matter. He's dead, anyway."

The car turned around and left, returning the way it had come. Caitlin felt paralyzed with shock. In all her experience, she had never witnessed anything so deliberately cruel and callous. Feeling a burning sensation in her chest, she realized she had forgotten to breathe.

Slowly drawing air into her lungs, she once again hurried down the hillside, surprised to notice that she was having no trouble distinguishing where she was going. Unnoticed, the sky had begun to lighten, signaling a new day.

Perhaps for the man who lay so still on the primitive roadway, there would never be a new day. A deep pain seemed to fill Caitlin's chest at the thought.

She was out of breath by the time she scrambled down to the road and dashed along its surface. There had been no movement from the man, and she was very much afraid there was nothing she could do for him.

As soon as she reached his side, she fell to her knees.

His skin was icy, and her heart sank. She felt for a pulse. The pounding of her heart seemed to shake her body with each beat. Her hand was shaking so much she couldn't find any sign of life.

She glanced around, trying to relate where she was with what she had witnessed happening. The man must have either jumped or been thrown from the car. His clothes were covered with dirt, and his features were all but obscured by blood. She got up from her knees and walked over to the edge of the road, peering over. The fire around the car seemed to have gone out, only the dark smoke curling up beside it evidence that there had been a blaze.

The poor man.

Why had the men been chasing him? Why had they wanted him dead? She wondered if she would ever know the answers.

In the meantime, what should she do? She couldn't leave him lying there while she went for help. It would take her hours. He needed help now, unless it was already too late. She needed to think calmly and rationally about what to do.

Slowly Caitlin walked back over to the man and looked down at him. She couldn't even see what he looked like, but she noted his tawny curls and waves, and winced. She didn't need to see his face to know who he was. He was the man she had seen earlier.

Making up her mind, Caitlin began to climb the mountain once again. She would bring Arturo down and attempt to take the man to the village.

Perhaps it was too late to save him, but he deserved a decent burial.

Decent. The word seemed to ring in her head. He had been a decent man. A kind man. A man who had not deserved to die on some lonely mountain road in the middle of nowhere.

By the time Caitlin reached Arturo, tears cascaded down her cheeks. There were many times when she found life particularly puzzling. Now was one of those times. Why had she seen him so clearly if she wasn't going to be given the opportunity to save him? What was the purpose of her being there?

She dried her eyes with the sleeve of her shirt. Whatever the reason, she was there, and she was going to see that he wasn't abandoned. Turning, she guided the burro back down the side of the mountain.

After positioning the burro beside the man, Caitlin discovered that he was much larger than she'd realized. She would have trouble getting him draped across the small animal without dragging his hands and feet; that is, if she could even lift him that far.

With infinite care and tenderness, she straightened the unknown man's legs and turned him so that he was lying on his back. She knelt and began to wipe the blood away from his face with one of the clean towels she always carried. The blood had come from a gash across his forehead, just beneath his hairline.

There was no expression on his face. He looked as though he were asleep, peacefully napping in the early morning light.

She felt a strange resonance inside her, as though a chord had been pulled. He had a beautiful face—clean, clearly defined, with high cheekbones and a strong jawline. His lips, in repose, looked as though they were made for smiling, and the slight lines around his mouth seemed to indicate he was a person who often found life amusing.

She sat and stared at him for a few moments until she realized she was wasting time. There was no reason to try to put off what had to be done.

Caitlin placed her arms around him, her head resting on his chest where his coat had fallen open, in an attempt to get him upright.

She froze, her eyes closing in a sudden spasm of excitement. An almost indiscernible rhythm reached her ear, which was pressed so close to his chest.

It was a heartbeat.

Two

—

Bright sunshine lit the clearing around Caitlin's small home by the time she and Arturo returned. She prayed that she would never experience such a harrowing morning again.

After leading the burro to the roadway, Caitlin had checked to make sure the man didn't have any broken bones. Then she had begun the task of lifting him.

Caitlin wasn't sure where she had found the strength to finally get the man onto Arturo's back. For the first time she fully understood what dead weight meant.

She'd been afraid of damaging the man even more by securing him on the small animal's back, so she had walked beside him, making sure his body didn't slide off.

Other than the thready pulse that she continued to monitor throughout their journey, he showed no signs of life, and she was gravely concerned. She had to keep reminding herself that at least he was alive, though barely. If she could get him back to the cabin, perhaps he had a chance.

Never had a place looked so good to her as her own clearing once they arrived. Caitlin didn't concern herself with the niceties of housekeeping at the moment. She led Arturo inside the cabin, despite his protests, so that she could slide the unconscious man onto the bed. Then she hurriedly returned Arturo to his stall, gave him the promised oats and ran back to the cabin.

The man hadn't moved. His skin felt clammy to the touch, and his gray color gave evidence to his state of shock.

"But you're alive," she whispered. "You're going to make it. Everything is all right. You're going to make it."

Searching in her bag for the small penlight she carried, Caitlin carefully lifted each of the man's eyelids, shining the light into his pupils and watching as they retracted slightly. The movement was sluggish, but at least there was some response, thank God. There was no doubt that he suffered from a concussion, possibly a skull fracture, but his brain was still functioning, at least to some degree.

The gash on his head no longer bled, and Caitlin knew she would have to stitch it, but not until she could clean and disinfect it.

First things first. She needed to get him out of his coat and boots, and try to make him more comfortable. From her quick check before she'd loaded him onto Arturo, the man had no broken bones, for which she was thankful. His head injury was serious enough.

Forcing herself to stay calm, Caitlin eased his heavy coat off his broad shoulders. The coat had cushioned his fall, probably saving him some cracked ribs. His Levi's had also taken the brunt of his fall. When she slipped his arm out of his coat sleeve, Caitlin flinched at the sight of the shoulder holster nestled securely under his arm.

She wondered how many law-abiding people wore shoulder holsters. *Or get run off the road, for that matter.* She forced herself to unfasten the holster and pulled it away from him. Caitlin knew nothing about guns. On purpose. She stared at the pistol lying in its holster and shivered. Glancing around the room, she didn't know what to do with it.

Was he dangerous? When he came to, would he try to kill her?

No. He was a decent man. Somehow she knew that, even though all other information she sensed seemed to be on the negative side. Whatever he was mixed up in was highly dangerous. She was a witness to that.

With sudden decision she wrapped the gun in a towel and hid it in her suitcase under the storage cabinet. Then she returned to the man lying unconscious on her bed.

After removing his boots, Levi's and shirt, she quickly covered him with blankets, then carefully bathed his face until it was clean. He looked so pale, and he lay there utterly still.

For the first time since she'd returned to the cabin, Caitlin became aware that the fire had gone out and that the room was cold. With the physical exertion she'd been going through all morning, she was almost perspiring, but she knew she had to get this man warm in a hurry. He had been unconscious for several hours, showing no sign of stirring.

Caitlin left him long enough to build another fire. Thank God the coals were still warm. She patiently waited while the kindling caught, then slowly and methodically added small twigs until flames began to dance once more.

Satisfied that the fire could be left on its own, Caitlin straightened slowly, her hand on the small of her back. She absently wondered what the stranger weighed. For a while that morning, her back felt as though she had broken it.

Checking him once again, she hoped that it wasn't her imagination that caused her to think his color was improving. His breathing was so shallow that she had trouble seeing any evidence of life, and she continually checked his pulse to make sure.

Pulling out a few herbs, Caitlin began to add them to some salve she had in a jar, mixing and stirring the concoction until she had the consistency she wanted. Then she returned to the bed and sat beside him.

He looked so peaceful. She traced his brow line, then his nose and jaw. If she were a sculptor, she'd be inspired to reproduce that face. Mentally reminding herself not to daydream, Caitlin began to bathe the man with sudsy warm water and blotted him dry, then covered each of his cuts and abrasions with the concoction she had mixed.

She carefully examined his face and the swelling on his forehead where he'd received a blow. She knew enough about head wounds to know that there was little she could do for him except prevent infection to the open wound. His body would have to heal itself.

After cleaning the gash on his forehead, she carefully stitched it closed, then covered the wound with the mixture of herbs and salve.

She stroked his cheek, where a day's growth of whiskers could be felt, but scarcely seen. His beard was as light as his hair.

"Your body needs time to heal, my friend," she said softly. "You are safe now. No one will harm you. Your body will take care of itself. You will rest and be comfortable. Everything is fine. You are safe."

She continued to sit there beside him, forcing her agitation to leave her and absorbing the calm serenity that always seemed to fill her cabin.

Caitlin couldn't remember the last time she had eaten. However, she knew she'd used up a considerable amount of energy since then. Humming softly, she prepared herself some lunch. She had finished and was washing up her dishes when she heard a soft tap at the door.

Visitors weren't too unusual since the local people thought of her as a healer. In addition, various people brought her food, items for the house and clothing in payment for her services.

She glanced over at the man in her bed. Of course, it was possible someone might be looking for him. She couldn't imagine who would possibly know to search for him here, but she couldn't afford to take any chances, not when she had witnessed an attempted murder.

Caitlin drew the homemade curtain that she had hung on a rod to divide the room in two, effectively concealing him from anyone standing at the doorway. She heard the soft tap again and strode over to the door and opened it.

She laughed. Her visitor wasn't human. "Well, good morning, Chula. Were you looking for me?"

A young deer stood there waiting. When the door opened, she walked inside the cabin with the familiarity of a long-established habit.

"I don't recall inviting you in, you know," Caitlin said with a grin, watching while the deer checked the dish near the fireplace. "Yes, I'm sure you're hungry. You're always hungry. What a panhandler."

Caitlin shook her head, closed the door and went over to the cabinet where she kept the grain. She poured some into the dish and held a small handful in her fist. Slowly opening her hand, she said, "Here you go, greedy."

The deer sniffed at the pan, then immediately moved toward her hand, daintily nibbling from her palm. "I can't believe how spoiled you are."

The spring before, Caitlin had found the deer not too far from the cabin, when it was still a wobbly-legged fawn with large spots and soulful eyes. Its dead mother had lain nearby.

The fawn had been too young and too hungry to know fear, and Caitlin had brought her home and kept her alive on goat's milk until she learned to eat.

Caitlin hadn't intended to make the animal a pet, but she didn't know what else she could have done. Now Chula, as Caitlin called her, had joined the group of animals that seemed to have found their home in and around Caitlin's clearing.

After Chula completed her meal, Caitlin coaxed her back outside. She paused in the doorway, looking up at the sun. What a beautiful day. Caitlin had trouble reconciling the violence she'd witnessed the night before with the peaceful serenity of the mountains and the sunshine.

Several birds swooped down from the trees and landed in a cluster at her feet. She stepped back into the cabin and gathered a double handful of food for them, then tossed it out. She sat down on the stoop and watched, unsurprised that several pecked their way over to her.

Her presence in the clearing had been accepted by the wildlife in ways she'd never fully understood. She'd just accepted it. They seemed unafraid. When she picked up a few sunflower seeds and placed them on her fingers, two of the birds nonchalantly lit on her palm and began to peck energetically.

She started laughing. "That tickles, you little beasts," she said, causing them to fly off, circle, then land back at her feet.

Caitlin went back inside and checked on her patient. He had not moved. However, she could see definite improvement in his breathing. His lungs seemed to be filling more deeply with air, so that his chest moved gently in rhythm.

Carefully tucking the covers around his neck once more, Caitlin decided to work on her loom. She found the steady rhythm of weaving the thread very soothing. Hopefully no one would need her today. She didn't want to leave the man alone, in case he regained consciousness.

Absently pushing the curtain back against the wall, Caitlin picked up what remained of his clothing. The shirt had fared well, since it had been protected by his jacket, and she thought the jeans were salvageable, although badly worn from his landing and rolling on the road. They would at least provide some covering for him once he was on his feet again.

She never allowed herself to think about him except as whole and healthy.

Picking up the jeans, she checked the pockets before placing them in the large kettle of steaming water that she used to wash her own things.

She found small change and a pocket knife in one of the front pockets, but that was all. She remembered the man hovering over his inert body. He must have taken his wallet.

He was a man with no identification. If he never came to, there would be no way to let anyone know what had happened to him.

Who was he?

For the first time since she'd regained consciousness in that Seattle hospital years ago, Caitlin wanted to utilize her unwanted skills: she wanted to solve the mystery of her new patient. Who was he, and why had someone tried to kill him?

She sat by the bed and studied him, letting her thoughts flow freely. Pictures began to form. She saw a woman with long blond hair, emerald-green eyes and a very provocative smile. Caitlin saw her run toward the man and throw her arms around him. They were both laughing.

There was another man, taller than her patient but built along the same lines: broad shoulders, narrow waist and hips, long well-muscled legs. She felt a close tie between the three people, a loving warmth that radiated between them. Caitlin knew with an inner certainty that those two people would be searching for the man who lay motionless beside her.

He was loved, this stranger, and Caitlin felt a moment of poignancy for the three people.

She reached over and lightly stroked his forehead. He felt warmer, as if his body were adjusting to its new environment. She folded one of the blankets away from him and studied his face. His color was definitely improving.

"You're going to be all right, my friend. You are safe now. No one will be able to find you and hurt you here. You are safe. Your body is healing."

And then what? Would he go out and try to get himself killed again? She knew better than to concern herself with future possibilities. Instead Caitlin focused her energies on getting him well.

She began to work at the loom quietly, periodically checking her patient for signs of consciousness.

By dark she felt ready to end her day. After feeding Arturo, her small group of chickens, the goat, and various wildlife that had grown used to coming in at dusk to feed, Caitlin returned to the cabin and lit one of her oil lamps.

She loved the soft glow the light gave to her home. In fact, she loved everything about the small cabin and gave thanks for the wisdom and determination she had needed to give up the life she had known to start over again in this unfamiliar wilderness. The move had been her salvation.

Caitlin glanced down at the man in her bed. Perhaps his salvation had also hinged on her move.

After getting ready for bed, banking the fire and replacing the fire screen, Caitlin came face-to-face with a decision she had unconsciously avoided all day. Where was she going to sleep?

The bed that Antonio had made for her was very large and would be more than adequate for the two of them. And what choice did she have? Short of curling up in her sleeping bag in front of the fire, she had none.

Leaning over the bed so that she could see his face, Caitlin knew that he would not know where she slept. With calm resolution, she lowered the wick on the lamp, leaving it lit so that she could see him if he should stir. Caitlin crawled into bed beside the stranger, and with a sigh of utter exhaustion, closed her eyes.

Within minutes she was asleep.

Caitlin lost track of time during the next several days. Her routine revolved around the unconscious man in her home. She watched him for signs of consciousness, sitting by the bed and talking to him, touching him, reassuring him in every way she knew that he would regain his strength and be all right.

Secretly she began to wonder. She was afraid to leave him in case he came to and she wasn't there. But she had a sense of danger connected with the village and wanted to check it out. Was it possible his assailants had returned and, not finding his body, realized he was alive? If so, his life could still be in jeopardy.

Caitlin awoke one morning with a feeling of renewed hope and optimism, refreshed and ready to face a new day. Her patient's color was good, and the angry wound showed signs of healing.

"Good morning," she said, as though he could hear her. "How are you feeling? I want to get some liquid down you today. I hope you will cooperate." She stood there and gazed at him, willing his eyes to open and meet hers, but she could see no response in his expression, not even a flicker of an eyelid.

Refusing to become discouraged, she turned away.

Chula entered the cabin as soon as Caitlin opened the door. Caitlin could see why Chula was so eager to be inside. A gray, heavily clouded sky swirled overhead, and she heard the wind whistling around the eaves.

"I suppose you intend to spend your day out of the weather," Caitlin said to Chula after she closed the door. The deer lay in front of the fireplace, her feet neatly tucked beneath her. Caitlin placed food in the bowl and poured some water into a small pan for her.

Quickly dressing in warm woolen pants and a hand-woven shirt, Caitlin made herself some breakfast and put a large pot of stew on the stove. Today she would attempt to feed her patient some broth.

She tried not to think about him as anyone other than a person who needed her help. But Caitlin had never known a man who affected her so strongly, not even Rick.

For almost a year she'd planned to marry Rick Shannon, thinking they had the perfect relationship. But Rick couldn't handle her ability to pick up on his thoughts and emotions after her near-brush with death. Eventually he had found a reason to terminate their engagement.

At the time she had been too immersed in her own grief at losing her parents to care. The very foundation on which her life had been built was gone. What did one more person leaving really mean to her?

Now she recognized that she had never loved Rick. She'd been in love with the idea of being in love. They had enjoyed the same pastimes, but the relationship had been very shallow. Caitlin felt lucky that they had found out before they had made the commitment to a marriage.

So why was she having such a strong reaction to this man? They had no relationship at all.

Are you sure? You saved his life, didn't you?

"That remains to be seen."

He would have died if you hadn't brought him back here.

"But he hasn't regained consciousness."

Give him time. His body needs time to restore itself.

"But when will he be aware of me?"

She received no answer.

Caitlin had never questioned the fact that she had brought him to her cabin. Neither she nor Arturo could have possibly managed to get him down the mountainside and to the settlement. She doubted the man would have survived the trip. He'd needed the warmth and quiet of her place almost as much as she had when she'd first moved there.

Now if he would only regain consciousness.

During the evening, she moved the lamp over closer to the bed and sat beside him. Taking his hand in hers, she said, "Please wake up. You need to eat something. You need to start moving around. Please open your eyes."

She stared at him, willing him to wake up. After several minutes she placed his hand on his chest and patted it. "Will you try for me?"

If she hadn't been studying his face so intently, she might have missed the slight flutter of his eyelashes. But because her hand was still lying on his, there was no way she could mistake the slight twitch of his thumb.

Tears filled her eyes. "Thank you" was all she could manage to say. Surely those weren't reflexes. He had heard her. She knew he had. And she needed to reassure him. "You're going to be all right. I know that now. You're going to be fine!"

Rushing over to the kitchen area, Caitlin began to spoon some broth into a bowl. The time had come to try to feed him. She laughed out loud.

He was going to be all right—she just knew it. He had to be.

Three

———

Caitlin watched him closely but saw no other signs that he might be regaining consciousness. However, she decided to talk to him as though he were awake and could hear her.

"I have some broth for you. You need the nourishment, and I'm sure you'll find it quite good. It's a recipe I invented since moving here. I throw whatever vegetables are available into the pot and let them cook for several hours. Why don't you try some?"

She sat down beside him with a cup of broth and dipped a spoon into the cup. Placing the half-full spoon on his lip, she gently inserted it between his teeth.

"Please swallow now. You mustn't choke." She set the cup down on the table beside the bed and massaged his neck while tilting the spoon slightly. She held her breath and waited.

Unmistakably she could feel the muscles in his neck as he swallowed. "You're wonderful—did you know that? I'm so proud of you." Quickly grabbing the cup, she dipped the spoon in once more. Caitlin lost track of the time she spent spooning the warm broth into his mouth. She refused to rush him. There was nothing she would rather do than to feed her patient as long as she could get him to take it.

After feeding him, she sponge bathed him and slipped his shirt back on. She needed to make him another one and, since there was no cloth she owned that would cover his broad shoulders, she knew she would have to weave a large skein of material. She would get started on that tomorrow, first thing.

Sometime later Chula stirred, and Caitlin let her outdoors, noting that the weather had not cleared. Since it was almost dark, she decided to feed the animals for the night and get ready for bed herself.

When she fell asleep that night, Caitlin was more and more encouraged with his progress. Although she had seen no further signs of returning consciousness during the past several hours, she was encouraged that he had been able to take some nourishment.

Caitlin slept heavily that night, her body and mind relaxing for the first time since she'd awakened with the sense of impending danger. The danger had been met, and hopefully, overcome.

The cabin grew colder as dawn approached, and in her sleep she drew closer to the warmth of the man beside her.

* * *

He kept hearing voices. Who were they, and what did they want? Sometimes they seemed to be whispering, and he strained to understand them.

One voice reoccurred, over and over. A soft, lilting voice that soothed him. Who was it?

"Felicia, is that you?"

No answer.

No, of course it wasn't Felicia. Felicia was in California while he was in—He was—Where? He was so confused. Was he at the ranch?

"Dane? Where are you?"

His body ached as though he'd been trampled by a herd of horses. And his head! Oh, God! He mustn't move his head, not at all. The slightest movement, and he fell back into that black pit of oblivion. Of course, there wasn't any pain there; he had to acknowledge that.

"But he couldn't stay there forever, could he?"

No. There was something he had to do. Right away. He'd worked hard for this meeting.

"Meeting? What meeting?"

Don't tell me you've forgotten the meeting. We were counting on you. Counting on you, counting on you.

The sound of a male voice close to her ear brought Caitlin from a sound sleep to a shocked wakefulness sometime later. What had she just heard?

Caitlin sat up in bed and stared at the man lying beside her. He was shifting restlessly, his head moving from side to side on the pillow. He was muttering something. She leaned closer to hear him.

"You don't understand. I can't move, I can't—"
His voice dwindled off into silence for a moment, then

came back even stronger. "Let me go, you bastards. Let me go!"

The words were muttered and slurred, but Caitlin could understand them. Whatever was happening in his mind had an urgency about it that he managed to convey in his voice and the tenseness of his body.

"Hello." Caitlin placed her hand on his forehead and smoothed the curls back. "Can you hear me?"

He quietened but didn't respond.

Caitlin got up and poured a small glass of water. Then she returned to the bed. "Would you like a drink?" She sat down beside him and lifted his head slightly by sliding her arm under the pillow. When she placed the glass to his lips, he opened his mouth and took a swallow.

For a moment Caitlin felt like weeping with relief. He wasn't fully conscious, but he was no longer in the seemingly lifeless state that had held him so still for the past several days.

After lowering him carefully, she put the glass down, then went over and built up the fire. Glancing out the window, she saw that dawn had arrived, although the cabin was still in shadows.

Humming to herself, she laid out the clothes she wanted to wear for the day. Then she grabbed her coat and pulled it over her nightclothes, put on her heavy walking boots and went outside to feed the animals and bring in more wood.

Chula followed her back into the cabin. She fed her, then poured some warm water into a bowl and hastily bathed herself before getting dressed. Caitlin stood before the fire, warming herself as she dressed.

* * *

Adam thought he was dreaming when he finally managed to focus his eyes. But where would his subconscious have picked up such a scene? He felt as though an oversize sledgehammer was continually tapping on his skull, and he found it difficult to concentrate.

The rustic cabin he seemed to occupy was small and immaculate, the furnishings sparse. Except for the statue of a small deer sitting on a rug in front of the fireplace, there was no ornamentation, unless he counted the woman standing before the large fireplace.

The glow from the fire tinted her skin apricot. She stood with her back to him, wearing a pair of panties that enticingly covered a deliciously curved derriere. Her long reddish-blond hair fell to her waist, the waves and curls beckoning him to run his hands through them.

He watched her as she dressed, unaware of him. Who was she? And what was he doing there?

Adam forced himself to concentrate, trying to ignore the throbbing pain in his head.

His last memory was standing in front of his hotel in Monterrey. Had he gone to a bar and been slipped something in his drink?

He studied the woman in front of him. She didn't look the type. Besides, he'd had something he had to do. What was it? Something important.

The throbbing pain increased when he frowned. He touched his forehead and felt a large welt that was extremely tender. His hand dropped to his jaw where he felt the roughness of a beard.

She turned toward him, reaching for her blouse. She had very delicate features. Her eyes were framed with dark lashes, and their blueness reminded him of a mountain lake.

"Who are you?" he said, his voice husky from disuse.

She grabbed her blouse to her breast in surprise, her expression startled as she stared at him from across the small space. Hastily turning her back to him, she tugged the shirt on over her head and pulled on a pair of jeans.

When she turned around again, her face was composed, but her color was heightened. Walking over to the bed, she sat down beside him and took his hand.

"I'm Caitlin," she said with a smile. "Who are you?"

The room kept receding from him. He blinked his eyes, trying to bring her into sharper focus. "Adam," he finally muttered, his throat dry.

"Adam," she repeated slowly, as though experimenting with the sound. At last she had a name for him. She liked it. Somehow it suited him. "You're going to be fine, Adam. You got a nasty blow to your head, but you'll be fine." She reached up and brushed his hair from his forehead in a familiar gesture, careful not to touch his wound.

He couldn't think. Her touch felt so soothing; it went with the sound of her voice. Her voice was so familiar, the tone as gentle as her touch... Adam drifted off to sleep, his breathing peaceful, his expression serene.

Time didn't seem to have any meaning to him, and he kept fading in and out of consciousness. He would open his eyes to daylight, close them, then reopen them to deep shadows that were only kept from engulfing him by a dim light somewhere nearby.

He was always aware of her presence. What had she said her name was? Caitlin, that was it. Caitlin with the soft voice and soothing hands.

Vaguely he was aware of her instructions to eat. From some far distant place she urged him to turn so that she could stroke him with a warm, wet cloth, its presence offering a balm to his aching body. He tried to tell her he could bathe himself, but somehow he couldn't find the words. *Takes too much concentration,* he decided.

Caitlin—beautiful angel of mercy and light, who kept the dark shadows away and soothed the pain that seemed to fill his body. How long had he known her? She seemed to be an integral part of his life. Had she always been there?

She smelled so good. Sometimes he would awaken in the darkness, his heart pounding, not knowing where he was, the ghost of a dream still swirling around him. Then her soft scent would reach him from somewhere close by, and he would remember where he was—that Caitlin was there—and he would relax.

Sometimes his dreams were filled with headlights relentlessly shining into his rearview mirror, looming closer and closer. Then he'd hear an explosion and feel as though he were flying through the air. But he never seemed to land.

Other times he dreamed of the ranch...of Felicia...of Dane. He kept trying to tell them he was all right and not to worry, but they never seemed to hear him.

He'd wake up in a cold sweat, trembling with the effort not to cry out with the pain that sometimes bit into his body and pulled him down to the pits of agony.

He became used to her touch, her soft scent, and a rhythmic thumping sound that he associated with her weaving. There were times when he would be aware of the stillness that was night. Once he woke up to find her sleeping curled up by his side. He smiled. Shifting slightly, he moved so that his hand could touch her arm. He found the closeness comforting.

Sometime during those many hours, Caitlin became a part of his thoughts, whether he was conscious or unconscious. Concentrating on her kept the pain from overwhelming him. Her presence kept the fear and confusion he was experiencing at bay.

Caitlin.

At last the day came when Adam could open his eyes and focus without the hazy double vision that had plagued him. He lay there quietly looking around the room that had somehow become familiar to him.

At first he didn't see Caitlin, not until she moved into his line of vision. Her reddish-blond hair hung in a single braid across her shoulder, resting on her breast. He smiled at the tranquil picture she made placing wood on the fire. She had become so much a part of him—an extension of who he was.

When she moved away from the fireplace, he tried to keep her in sight by turning his head. He immediately discovered his mistake when the pain in his head magnified. Adam must have made some sort of noise, because Caitlin glanced up, and when she saw him watching her, she smiled, an enchanting smile that made her eyes sparkle.

"How do you feel?" she asked, walking over to the bed and taking his hand in hers.

"Like my head's been used for batting practice a few too many times," he managed to say. His voice sounded almost rusty. "Where are we?" he asked, his curiosity finally piqued enough to inquire.

"The mountains."

She made her answer sound so simple, as though he should know that. There were no mountains anywhere near the ranch, just rolling hills.

"Are we in Texas?"

She chuckled, shaking her head. "No. Mexico."

Mexico. What the hell was he doing in Mexico? "What am I doing here?"

"You were in an accident not too far from here and badly injured. Since there's no town nearby, I brought you to my home to help you recover."

He thought about that for a moment but could think of nothing else to ask. He knew he was hurt. He'd never felt so much pain before.

Her hand continued to hold his firmly. Carefully moving his eyes so that the pain wouldn't increase, he studied their clasped hands. His was large and work-roughened, wide, with a callused palm. Hers was dwarfed next to his, her fingers long and slender, and very pale, like the rest of her.

He glanced up and became aware of her expression. She was smiling as though immensely pleased with him. He idly wondered why. He couldn't have been much company lately.

"How long have I been here?" *Forever, surely. Was there ever a time when you and I weren't together?*

"I'm not sure, exactly. I'm afraid I lost track of time . . . you've been so ill."

Not that it mattered. He was content to lie there looking at her while she held his hand. He could look at her all day, every day, and not grow tired of her face, her very lovely, expressive face.

Caitlin was touched by the tender expression he wore. Touched and slightly alarmed. He mustn't grow attached to her. She felt the inner warning that she was too late—her loving care of him had created a bond between them. After several moments of silence, she realized she needed to distract him.

"Where do you live, Adam?" she asked, unobtrusively releasing his hand and folding hers together on her lap.

Adam had to think about her question for a moment. He felt as though all the moving parts of his brain were buried in gallons of molasses and responded sluggishly whenever he tried to think. He found it much easier to let his mind wander and just to enjoy his sensory perceptions. He missed the touch of her hand.

Frowning slightly, he tried to concentrate on her question. His home. Where was it? "On a ranch . . . in Texas. Near Mason." His eyes sought hers. "Do you know where that is?"

He watched her as she shook her head. That was all right. He'd show her someday, when he felt better. He would take her back to the ranch, let her meet Dane and his neighbors and friends. Maybe he could convince Felicia to fly home for a visit. He knew the two women would enjoy each other.

"What are you doing here in Mexico, Adam?"

Good question. He frowned once again, trying to force his brain to work. His thoughts continued to swim around inside his head without rhyme or reason.

Car lights shining in the rearview mirror. He'd been going somewhere, meeting someone.... Danger. What he was doing was dangerous.

With a sudden start Adam felt along his side.

"Where's my pistol?"

She nodded toward the corner. "I put it in my suitcase, where it would be safe," she assured him.

The pistol didn't need to be safe. *They* needed to be safe. They would be safer if he had the gun nearby; didn't she understand that? Maybe she didn't.

"How long have I known you?"

Unconsciously Caitlin reached for his hand once more and she began to stroke his knuckles with her other hand. "Just since the accident."

"You don't know why I'm here?"

"Not very clearly, I'm afraid. I've picked up that you were on your way to meet someone, someone important to you, and you never made it."

"What do you mean, you picked up?"

Her grip on his hand tightened, and he watched several expressions move across her face. He wanted to tell her that it didn't matter and that he didn't want to cause her pain.

"I see pictures in my head," she said in a hesitant voice. "That's how I knew about you, that you were nearby, that you would be hurt."

She wasn't making much sense. But then, nothing made much sense to him at the moment.

"You mean my accident."

"Yes, except what happened to you wasn't an accident. You were forced off the road and almost killed."

Bright lights reflected in a rearview mirror, almost blinding him... Yes. He remembered now. He didn't know where they came from. Suddenly they were behind him, coming up fast, and he had no place to go to get out of their way—except down the side of the mountain.

Adam tried to put everything she had told him into some coherent form. An accident that he could only remember in snatches. An accident that wasn't an accident. She had been there. She... "You saved my life," he said, speaking his thoughts aloud.

Caitlin felt as though she were drowning in the gray-green eyes that gazed up at her. The pain he was still experiencing was apparent. She wanted to hold him to her and comfort him as though he were a child. But this man was no child. Not in any way.

"I'm glad I was able to," she managed to say.

They studied each other in silence for a while, that invisible bond drawing them closer.

Adam's thoughts seemed to drift—away from Caitlin, away from the cabin. He stirred restlessly. "Somehow I have to tell them—"

"I know. There are people who need to know that you're alive," Caitlin responded, understanding his concern. "But they will wait, Adam. First you need to mend."

His eyes drooped shut. "So tired."

Without considering her actions, she leaned down and kissed his cheek. "I know. Go to sleep now. You have plenty of time." Her voice was carefully modulated and very soothing. "Now is the time to rest. You'll feel better soon. The worst is behind you."

Adam smiled at her touch. He loved her soft scent, her warm touch, her tranquil presence nearby. He loved...

The next time he opened his eyes the room was in shadows, with only the glow of the fireplace illuminating the small home. Once again Adam's gaze sought out the woman who seemed to fill all of his thoughts, both waking and dreaming. She sat in a small rocker before the fire, doing handwork.

"Do you live here alone?" he asked, destroying the silence of the room.

Caitlin glanced around and stood up. Coming over to his side, she automatically touched his hand, then his cheek. "Not totally. Chula keeps me company from time to time." She nodded to the deer statue in front of the fireplace.

Adam frowned, wondering if she had been alone too long.

She left his side and went to the kitchen area where she picked up a small bag. Returning to the fireplace, Caitlin reached her hand into the bag and pulled out some oats, placing them in a small bowl he hadn't noticed before.

His eyes widened when the statue unfolded its legs and got up, stepping daintily across the rug to the bowl where it began to eat.

He began to understand how Alice must have felt when she stepped through the looking glass.

Caitlin brought him a bowl of stew and sat down beside him. He started to take the bowl and discovered his arms felt weighted.

"There's no reason for you to exert yourself just yet. Why don't you just relax and let me feed you?"

The idea held considerable merit. Adam relaxed against the pillows and obligingly opened his mouth whenever she brought the spoonful of food toward him.

He continued to study her—enjoying the sight of her fair skin, her softly rounded cheek, her small, straight nose, the shape of her finely molded mouth. Although she pretended to ignore his scrutiny, a soft rose coloring washed across her cheeks. Adam was delighted to see her reaction. No matter how she tried, she couldn't pretend that they were strangers. Never that.

When he finished the last spoonful of food, Caitlin stood up. "Why don't you rest now?"

Adam frowned. "All I do is sleep."

"I know," she said sympathetically. "But it's the best thing for you. You're making excellent progress, you know."

His mind returned to the cause of his injuries.

"Did you see what happened to me?"

Caitlin nodded, her expression somber.

"Tell me what you saw. Everything you can remember."

After rinsing out the bowl, she returned to his side. Once again she took his hand, unobtrusively keeping watch over his pulse. He didn't need to get upset. But keeping what happened from him might be just as upsetting. As briefly as possible, Caitlin explained the sequence of events she had witnessed.

When she fell silent, Adam lay there, staring into space. Two men tried to kill him. Why? Were they hoping to keep him from making contact with the possible informer? How had they known about the meeting?

And just as important—how was he going to find them?

"Did you get a look at the men?"

"Not a clear look, no, but I would know them again if I saw them."

He wished he understood how Caitlin had known what was going to happen to him. How could she identify two men she'd only seen in the dark? He couldn't deny that there was something different about her—something that had led her to him. How had she known?

Wearily Adam closed his eyes, trying to crowd out the pain that seemed to engulf him every time he tried to concentrate. Rest. He needed to rest. Adam kept hoping that his patience would be rewarded and the pain would go away.

Adam drifted off to sleep once more.

Caitlin watched him for a long time, grateful to see that he was resting easier. She had added a tea that she had brewed to the food she had given him. Hopefully the tea would help to combat the pain he was experiencing without creating any other problems for him.

With any luck at all, he would sleep through the night. She smiled to herself, wondering what she would do if he woke up sometime and found her by his side? Once he was awake more, she would get the sleeping bag out and sleep in front of the fire. She didn't want to encourage him to think she wanted anything more from him.

Caitlin had been aware of his thoughts earlier. He was attracted to her, just as she was attracted to him. But the attraction would be better if left unacknowledged. His life existed outside of the mountains. She had no desire to ever leave them, not even to be somewhere nearer to Adam.

She already knew that Adam would hold a very special place in her heart. And why not? A person didn't save another person's life every day, she tried to tell herself. But she knew better. Her work with the villagers had already shown her how valuable she had become in the area where she lived.

Adam was different. She just had to keep in mind that there could be nothing between them.

Caitlin lay awake for several hours that night, thinking of the man sleeping so soundly beside her. There was a reason he'd come into her life, a lesson she would learn from the experience. She only hoped the lesson wasn't accompanied with more pain than she could handle.

Adam awoke early, and Caitlin quickly prepared a nourishing meal for him. They talked for a while, with Caitlin choosing light subjects that took little effort on Adam's part. She teased him about his good looks, then found herself embarrassed when he returned her teasing with interest.

She helped him to sit up on the side of the bed for a few moments, then helped him to stretch out once more when he showed definite signs of fatigue. Sleep overcame him once more, and she was free to continue her daily routine.

While waiting for her patient to awaken later in the afternoon, Caitlin decided to make bread. Baking was another soothing task for her. She particularly enjoyed the smell the freshly baked bread gave to her small home. She hummed while she worked, content.

When Adam awakened again, his head was much clearer than it had been. Glancing out the window, he was surprised to see that night had fallen while he had slept. The cabin was filled with shadows except for the firelight and an oil lamp that sat on a table near a hand loom where Caitlin was working. The thump of the shuttles was a familiar sound he'd grown accustomed to.

The small room smelled of fresh bread. For all he knew, he could be in another century. The surprising thing was that it didn't matter. He felt at peace with the world and all the creatures in it.

If only the ache in his head would let up. The pain was a constant companion. He couldn't seem to remember a time when the steady throbbing hadn't coursed through him.

God! He felt so helpless.

He attempted to turn on his side, causing the throbbing in his head to increase alarmingly, and he groaned.

Caitlin immediately got up and moved to the side of the bed. "I didn't realize you were awake," she said, noting the tension in his face. "I have something ready for you that should help the pain."

He nodded slightly, acknowledging her words. His teeth were clamped together, as though he were afraid that if he tried to speak he would not be able to with-hold another groan.

Caitlin poured a cup of the herbal tea she'd pre-pared and brought it over to him. "It should still be warm," she said, skillfully lifting his head with the pillow and holding the cup to his mouth.

Adam drank the warm liquid, making a face. His gaze sought hers. She was only a few inches away, and he saw tiny gleams of gold deep within the blue of her eyes. He'd never seen a color quite like that before.

"What was that?" he muttered.

She smiled. "You must be feeling better. You're sounding grouchy. The tea is a mixture of herbs that I grow—it should help ease your pain."

"I don't think you need to worry about Lipton trying to steal your formula."

Her chuckle sounded husky and warm. "Probably not."

She put the empty cup down and looked at him for a moment. "We really need to get you up again, if you think you can manage."

She watched as a dull redness filled his cheeks. "I'd prefer getting up to your taking care of me."

Caitlin knew what he meant, but she wasn't sure he could manage on his own. "It's outside, you know."

Without meeting her eyes, he nodded. "I figured as much."

"It's not far, if you'd like me to help you."

"For some reason, the idea of your helping me doesn't improve my self-image at all."

Their gazes finally met, and they both began to laugh at their mutual embarrassment. Adam clutched his head in dismay as the pain accelerated.

"I meant I'd help you walk out there," Caitlin explained, absently stroking his forehead as though to ease the pain. "You're going to be very weak."

Between the two of them, he managed to sit on the side of the bed. For the first time Adam registered the fact that he was only wearing his shirt and briefs. What had he expected, anyway? Hadn't she bathed him and looked after him when he was too helpless to even lift his head?

He glanced up and met her eyes but didn't say anything. She handed him his jeans and watched as he struggled to pull them on. He was mortified by the weakness. Adam had always been healthy and vigorous, and work on the ranch had given him stamina and endurance. Now he could feel himself trembling after no more exertion than sitting up and pulling on a pair of jeans!

She placed a pair of homemade slippers on his feet and helped him to stand.

By the time he was on his feet, he was more than willing to drape his arm around her shoulders for support. "I'm sorry your coat took such a beating," she said, her head braced against his shoulder. "I tried to clean it for you, but I don't think it will ever be the same." She had forgotten what a large man he was until now, when he was on his feet.

"Don't worry about it," he muttered. Beads of perspiration formed on his forehead, and Caitlin felt the effort he made to concentrate as he forced himself to walk to the door, wait for her to open it, then step outside.

Thankfully they didn't have far to go. She helped him open the door, then discreetly walked away and waited until he opened it again. His color was pasty white, and she knew it was only through sheer force of will that he managed to return to the cabin.

Adam stretched out on the bed once more with a sigh, his eyes closed. She pulled the slippers off his feet, glad that she had taken the time to make them for him while he'd been unconscious. Neither one of them would have been able to get his boots on.

She studied him for a moment in silence. He needed to take off his coat as long as he was inside. He'd fallen asleep—exhausted from the exertion—and she knew that without his cooperation, she would have a difficult time.

Nevertheless, she managed to tug the sleeves off, then rolled him slightly so she could pull the coat out from under him. He never stirred.

The herbal mixture would not only ease the pain but once again ensure a good night's sleep.

Caitlin hadn't realized how late it was. She'd become hypnotized by her weaving. She almost had enough material now to make Adam a shirt—tomorrow she would cut it out.

Going through her nightly ritual of checking the animals, banking the fire and dressing for bed, Caitlin realized that she had become used to sleeping with Adam. The cabin would seem so empty when he was gone.

Blowing out the light, she quietly crawled into bed beside him. Touching his face, she was relieved to feel his natural warmth. Thank God his getting up for those few minutes didn't seem to have caused any aftereffects. The next step was getting him on his feet for longer periods of time, so that he could slowly start gaining back his strength.

She had done her job. Adam was definitely on the mend. Soon he would be strong enough to leave.

Caitlin wasn't sure why she found the thought unsettling.

Four

———

As the days slowly passed, Adam's returning strength became apparent. He stayed up for longer periods of time now than he was in bed. Adam found a quiet pleasure in following Caitlin around as she worked outside, feeding the burro, milking the goat, gathering eggs, as well as feeding half the wildlife in the mountains.

He was surprised to discover the number of people who called on her, either to bring her items in payment for her assistance or to ask for some of her herbal remedies.

At first the local people were shy around him, whispering among themselves whenever they happened to see him watching them. But as the days passed, they seemed to take the presence of the tall, quiet Texan for granted.

He heard one of the women teasing Caitlin about him one day, referring to him as her sweetheart. Caitlin glanced around to see if Adam had heard the woman, quickly denying any relationship.

He wondered if the tension between them was so obvious to outsiders. Adam couldn't control his reactions to Caitlin. They seemed to have always been there inside of him, waiting to be released. The more he learned about her, the more he delighted in her.

Yet he knew so little about her. He just knew he loved her with a quiet intensity that seemed to grow with every day that passed.

Why was she living alone in the mountains? Whenever they talked, she guided the subject away from herself and asked no questions about him. Didn't she care at all about who he was and why he was in Mexico? As the days passed, Adam found himself filled with questions he couldn't answer.

On one rather warm day Adam sat outside in the sunshine and watched while Caitlin worked in her garden, preparing it for spring planting.

Spring. It certainly felt that way today. He wondered how long he'd been there and why the urgency for him to leave seemed to have disappeared.

He knew that several weeks had gone by. The weather had warmed considerably since he first came to Mexico. No doubt everyone knew he was missing by now. Why had no one come looking for him?

Maybe they had. How could anyone have found him sitting up here on a mountainside? He would have to find a way back to Monterrey. Soon. Very soon. But not today.

Adam glanced up at the sound of Caitlin's laughter. Chula was nudging her with her nose, trying to get her attention. He smiled at the picture she made, playing with the deer. She seemed so content with her life, so innocent in many ways. As though none of life's ills had ever touched her. As though she lived in a magical forest created by Disney and populated with endearing creatures.

She was different from anyone he had ever known. A very special person. What was it she had told him when he'd first regained consciousness? Something about seeing pictures in her mind, knowing when something was going to happen?

What was that called? There was a word for it. Psychic. She was psychic.

Caitlin never talked about it, but then he'd never brought the subject up again. It was as though a barrier appeared between them at the thought of discussing her psychic abilities. Then again, she just might be shy about it. Maybe he'd question her about her strange abilities sometime.

Sometime.

How much longer would he need to stay with her before his body wouldn't betray him with its weakness?

Adam hated the thought of leaving her there on the mountaintop and returning to his world alone. He kept picturing her at the ranch, making pets of all the horses and having Chula trailing along behind her. Adam smiled at the thought.

"Caitlin?"

The sound of his voice seemed to startle her, and she jumped. "Yes?" She walked over to where he sat on a log. He had shaved that morning for the first time, and Caitlin couldn't control her reaction to his handsome good looks. She tried to cover her feelings by saying, "All you need is a sombrero, and you'd be part of the land of *mañana*." He smiled, silently acknowledging his indolent position.

"That's what I wanted to talk to you about. I need to get some exercise. Could we take a short walk, do you think?"

She glanced around the clearing, aware of the warmth and sunshine that was helping to heal him. Looking back at him, she smiled. "Sure. If you think you're up to it."

Adam stood up, stretched, then dropped his arm companionably around her shoulder. "Well, there's no time like the present to find out."

"Where would you like to go?" she asked.

"How about showing me where you found me?"

She shook her head. "I really think that's too far for you to walk. But we can start out in that direction."

Adam soon discovered what she meant. The terrain was rugged, and he could scarcely believe she had been able to bring him back in his unconscious state.

He was more than ready to rest when she suggested they take advantage of an outcrop of rock to sit down. "Don't you ever get lonely living up here?" he asked after they had sat in silence for a while.

"Loneliness is a state of mind. The loneliest time of my life occurred when I lived in a large city."

"Ah—so you didn't suddenly appear here on the planet and choose this place to reside."

She laughed at his whimsy.

"I'm afraid not. Is that what you thought?"

"I've never met anyone like you. I'm not sure what to think."

She grinned impishly at him. "I take it you're not used to people who know what you're thinking."

He stared at her for a moment, then shook his head. "Sorry, I can't buy that one. I'm still trying to get used to the idea you saw what happened to me before it actually occurred."

Caitlin gazed out over the vista of mountains and trees. When she spoke, her voice was soft. "You've been trying to figure a way to ask me to go home with you."

Her quiet words caught him unprepared and he looked at her with a startled expression. Before he could comment, she continued. "The feelings you've been having about me are very natural, Adam, but don't mistake gratitude for something else. What you're feeling will eventually be forgotten once you're back home in familiar surroundings."

"How do you know what I'm thinking and feeling?" he demanded.

"Partly because I was once very ill myself. It's easy to become dependent on those who are caring for you. Your world shrinks to the very basics of existence. Everyone in that world assumes a tremendous importance to your well-being."

"You think that's why I'm attracted to you?" he asked, unconsciously acknowledging his feelings. "It couldn't have anything to do with the fact that I find you very attractive, could it?"

"I know there's a sexual awareness between us. It's very strong."

"But you don't intend to do anything about it, do you?"

"No."

Adam ran his hand through his already rumpled hair. "You refuse to see me as anything other than your patient, is that it?"

"I believe that's the wisest course to follow, yes."

"And you're always so wise," he said in a sarcastic tone.

She laughed. "Now you're feeling like a little boy who was told that candy would spoil his supper."

Adam grinned reluctantly. "I suppose you're right, at least partly. You sound so damned sure of yourself—talking as though feelings can just be brushed aside and forgotten."

"I'm sorry. That isn't what I mean. I just think we both need to recognize that we come from different worlds. It's better not to get too involved."

"What's wrong with my world?"

"Nothing," she replied.

"Then why do you avoid it?"

"I learned that the world you live in is too painful for me."

"In what way?"

"People don't want their thoughts and emotions revealed and understood. They need their masks to face life."

"Only people who have something to hide, perhaps," he offered thoughtfully.

"We all have something to hide."

Adam felt tenderness for Caitlin well up within him at the pensive expression on her face. "What do you hide, Caitlin?" he asked softly.

"Fear," she said after a moment. "Fear of rejection. Fear of being hurt."

"So you stay up here on your mountainside where you're safe."

"Yes."

He stood up and held out his hand. "Let's go home."

They were quiet on the return trip, absorbed in their thoughts.

Adam felt that he had taken the first step in understanding her a little better. He didn't care how she tried to explain his feelings away. He knew they were based on more than gratitude. He just wasn't sure what he was going to do about them.

The next morning, Adam was sitting at the table and had just finished his breakfast when Caitlin came up behind him and began to stretch a tape across his shoulders.

"What are you doing?" he asked, turning around in surprise.

"Getting your measurements. I'm making you a shirt."

Obligingly he stood up and held out his arms with a grin. "I've never had a custom-made shirt before."

"Obviously deprived," she said with an answering smile, writing something down.

"That's better than being depraved," he offered solemnly.

She glanced up at him with a puzzled expression.

He explained. "What if you had discovered once you got me back to your home that I was some sort of monster who would attack you when I recovered?"

"I wasn't worried," she replied. "I had Chula here to protect me."

They both looked over at the deer curled up asleep on the rug in front of the fireplace and grinned at each other.

Adam walked over to the door and looked out. "Think I'll chop some wood. That should help to rebuild some of my strength."

Caitlin watched him leave with something like relief. Each day it was becoming more of a trial to act relaxed and unconcerned when she was around Adam.

She knew as well as he did that what he felt toward her was more than gratitude. The thought of his falling in love with her scared her to death—because she had already faced the truth of her own feelings for him.

She loved Adam.

Who wouldn't? He had a gentleness of spirit that disarmed her, a sense of the ridiculous that kept her entertained, an integrity that shone like a beacon from his eyes. Most men would have resented anyone seeing them as weak and vulnerable as Adam had been at first. Yet he was sure enough of himself to accept his limitations as temporary and not take out any feelings of inadequacy on her.

Caitlin could see his strength slowly grow with each day that passed. Soon he would be well enough to hike down the mountainside. Then he would be gone.

Not once did she consider going with him. She had learned her lesson with Rick. No one could be comfortable living with a person like her.

Adam stayed outside most of the day. The weakness that tired him so quickly seemed to drag on day after day. When he finally went inside, he found the shirt Caitlin had made for him draped over his chair.

She was outside feeding her animals. They hadn't spoken much that day. They didn't seem to need words to communicate. A glance, a shrug, a smile—all seemed to add to the intimacy they had unwittingly established.

Adam sighed.

He was definitely on the mend. His body could attest to that. Just thinking about her created certain body changes that were uncomfortable as well as embarrassing. He had never wanted another woman the way he wanted Caitlin, and yet he had never even kissed her.

Since he'd moved out of her bed—he smiled when he remembered the night that had happened—they had carefully avoided physical contact, as though by unspoken agreement. Perhaps that was why her hands had seemed to scorch his shoulders that morning when she measured him for the shirt he was now holding.

He sat down at the table, thinking about the night when he'd seen her dragging out a well-used sleeping bag.

"What are you doing?" he'd asked, frowning.

She glanced around at him, surprised at his tone. "Going to bed. Why?"

"You don't have to sleep on the floor."

Caitlin registered no expression when she replied. "Yes, I do."

"Since when? You've seemed to rest quite comfortably curled up by my side each night."

He watched as a lovely flow of color spread over her face. "I didn't realize you knew I was there," she murmured.

He walked over to her. "Knowing you were there kept the nightmares away. I thought you knew."

Her gaze didn't quite meet his. "Well, you're not having nightmares any longer."

He took her hand and studied her palm as though preparing to give her a reading. Without looking up, he said, "But I might, if you weren't there."

She pulled her hand away as though it had been burned. "Then you'll have to deal with it. I'm not going to sleep with you."

The smile he gave her was full of mischief. "If you don't want to sleep, I'm sure we can find something to do to while away the hours."

She whirled away from him and knelt on the sleeping bag.

Adam spoke again. "If anyone's going to bed down on the floor, it will be me."

She must have heard the calm determination in his voice because she looked up at him with dismay. "You won't be able to sleep down here. And you need your rest, Adam."

He'd continued to look at her until she'd gotten up and reluctantly walked over to the bed.

Adam stared at the shirt in his hand now as he sat at the table. She had worked all day to make it for him.

Why? Why was she so willing to give her time and energy—not only to him but to anyone who needed her? Yet she was not willing to give her emotions, or herself. What had happened that had caused her to retreat from the world? He didn't know, and he couldn't leave until he had some answers; Caitlin had become too important to him. Adam had begun to face the fact that she had unobtrusively found her way into his heart. He wasn't going to be able to forget her—not now.

Adam had no choice but to try to understand this woman. He couldn't help but wonder if it would do him any good.

Adam lay in front of the fireplace late that night staring into the flickering flames, unable to sleep. From the corner of the room he heard the quiet rustling of covers and knew Caitlin was no more asleep than he was.

"Caitlin?"

"Yes."

"Can't you sleep?"

There was a short silence, then a sigh. "Not really. Can you?"

"No."

"Would you like me to make us something to drink?"

"Sounds good to me."

He heard her stirring, getting out of bed. He pictured what she was doing by the sounds she made. He could hear her pour water into a pan, stoke up the stove, hear the clatter of cups. After a while she appeared beside him, holding out a cup to him.

He sat up, taking the cup, and watched her sit down in the rocking chair nearby. Caitlin wore her heavy velour robe with a hood that she had pulled around her head. The navy blue folds emphasized the red of her hair and the fairness of her complexion. She gazed at the fire in quiet contemplation and Adam felt a calmness seep through him now that he could see her.

"Have you ever been in love, Caitlin?"

If his abrupt question startled her, she didn't show it. Slowly her gaze moved from the mesmerizing flames until her eyes met his. With a slight smile she said, "I thought I was ... once."

"Tell me about it."

Perhaps it was the late hour and the fact that they could only see each other by the light of the fire. Whatever the reason, Caitlin felt comfortable, even protected, as though she were functioning in a dream state.

"Rick and I met in high school and dated during our last two years there. We became engaged our sophomore year of college." Her gaze returned to the fire. "We were both only children and spoiled—although neither of us were aware of that, of course. We'd had happy childhoods: things had always happened the way we wanted them to. We saw no reason why we couldn't expect our plans to continue to work out as we envisioned them. We were going to marry after graduation, wait three years to have children—"

She suddenly stopped speaking. Adam waited. Eventually she lifted her hand and made a slight dismissing gesture.

"It didn't work out that way."

After several minutes of silence Adam relaxed on his sleeping bag, his arms folded behind his head. "Did he find someone else?" he asked in a quiet voice.

She shrugged, never taking her eyes off the dancing flames. "The accident ended everything."

"What sort of accident?"

"Mom, Dad and I had been to the King Dome to watch a football game. We were on our way home when we were hit head-on by a speeding car whose driver was attempting to outrun a police car. I happened to be in the back seat. The doctors say that was the only thing that saved me. They say Mom was killed instantly and Dad died a few hours after arriving at the hospital."

"My God!"

"I was in a coma for several weeks. When I began to come out of it I 'saw' the accident happen, as though I was a witness to it. Then I 'watched' Rick when he heard the news of the accident. I saw him visit me in the intensive care unit while I was unconscious and felt his revulsion at the sight of me."

"Is that when you developed your psychic abilities?"

"I didn't develop them. They were just there after the accident. When I regained consciousness, I knew what the doctors were going to say before they said it. More importantly, I knew what they weren't saying."

She glanced down at Adam lying on the floor near her feet and for a moment couldn't remember what she had been saying. The light from the fire shed a golden glow over his upper body, lovingly outlining the planes and hollows as he lay there, his cover carelessly pushed to his waist. She couldn't see his eyes but felt their gaze on her.

Her thoughts changed course abruptly, and she wondered why she was telling him about her past. She'd never talked about it with anyone before.

Caitlin shook her head in confusion.

"How did Rick take the change in you?" Adam asked in a matter-of-fact tone.

"He was appalled when he discovered that I could tell what he was thinking and feeling, particularly when it was a contradiction to what he was saying. He denied it, said I was making up everything as an excuse to break up with him. That's when I knew my relationship with Rick was over, and that at the very best of times, it had been very shallow and one-dimensional."

Adam found himself thankful that the relationship had ended, then felt a flash of guilt because he knew how she must have suffered. "What happened then?"

"Eventually I was well enough to go home. Only there was no home for me. Certainly not in the house where I'd spent my entire life with my parents." Caitlin stared into the fire, seemingly lost in her memories. In a low voice she continued, "I couldn't deal with all the changes taking place around me, as well as all the internal confusion I was experiencing at the time."

Slowly turning her gaze until she focused on Adam's face, she searched for the words to try to explain what she had never attempted to express before. "The most difficult part was trying to relate to the people all around me. I could no longer tolerate crowds. Everyone's thoughts and feelings seemed to bombard me and I would go home feeling emotionally bruised and battered."

Adam could see the strain that discussing her past was causing Caitlin. He also sensed that she needed to talk about it—to face it and come to terms with it. He waited patiently for her to continue.

Finally she said, "I didn't understand what had happened to me. I was not only trying to come to terms with my grief, but I was also convinced I was losing my mind."

They sat in silence, and Caitlin realized that she was experiencing a sense of security she hadn't felt since her parents' deaths.

Adam rolled over on his side and propped himself up on one elbow. "I don't believe you were losing your mind. In my line of work our intuitive powers have oftentimes been the only thing that saved us." He absently toyed with the clasp on the zipper of the sleeping bag, flicking it back and forth with his finger. "Obviously your abilities were enhanced in some manner not easily explainable. But that doesn't make them any less real."

For the first time since his arrival, Adam had given her an opening to ask him some questions of her own.

"What is your line of work, Adam?"

He smiled. "I assumed you'd already figured that out."

"I know that you're not what you appear to be. You have a secret life that few people know about. That you're a decent, honest man, but you don't let many people get close to you." She wondered how much she could say without offending him. Hesitating briefly, she added, "There's a wall around you, an emotional wall, that no one would dare try to scale."

Adam's eyes narrowed slightly at her words, but his expression didn't change. "I can see why your friends would be uneasy around you. A person can't have any secrets from you."

She sensed a hint of hostility, which didn't surprise her. She had grown used to that sort of reaction.

"I don't know why you carry a gun," she pointed out with a smile.

He studied her in silence for a few moments. She had responded to his probing questions, despite the pain the answers had caused her. He owed her nothing less than a complete and honest response to her questions.

Adam shifted slightly, aware of the floor's hard surface despite the padding of the rug and sleeping bag.

"Before I can explain that," he finally said, "I need to fill you in a little on my background." He paused for a moment, gathering his thoughts. "The St. Clair ranch has been in my family for several generations," he began slowly. "I was just a kid when my dad died, leaving my mom, sister and I to run the place." His eyes sought hers. "Thank God we had a dependable foreman, or we'd never have made it. Mom died when I was a teenager, and I became responsible for my sister, Felicia."

Now Caitlin had an opportunity to satisfy her curiosity. "Is she tall, blonde, with green eyes?"

Adam looked startled for a brief moment, then grinned. "That's her."

"And she's in love with the man who runs the ranch with you?"

Adam abruptly sat up. "Dane Rineholt?"

"Is he part owner of the ranch?"

Slowly Adam relaxed, staring at Caitlin with something close to dismay. Her abilities were definitely unsettling at times. "Yes," he said, "as a matter of fact he is. He became my partner several years ago. What with low beef prices and a drought, I almost lost the ranch until he came along." In a musing tone he added, "So Felicia's in love with Dane. That explains a lot."

"Didn't you know?" she asked, surprised that he hadn't been aware of something that came to her so clearly.

"I had my suspicions," he admitted. "I'd never seen Felicia react so strongly toward someone the way she did to him. At times I was convinced she hated him. I wonder if he knows how she feels?"

"Yes, I think he does." In her mind, she saw them together. "Is Felicia at the ranch now?"

Adam shook his head. "Not that I know of. As far as I know, she's in Los Angeles. She works for a magazine there."

Caitlin could see Felicia at the ranch and for a moment felt the tremendous grief experienced by the other woman. Felicia thought Adam was dead. Her love for her brother was graphically portrayed by the depth of her suffering. She must have come home when she heard Adam was missing.

"She loves you very much," she murmured.

"No more than I love her." He stood up, and Caitlin stiffened until she realized he still wore his jeans, even though he was shirtless and barefoot. Adam placed more wood on the fire, his movements making the muscles in his arms and shoulders ripple under the smooth expanse of his skin.

He's beautiful, Caitlin thought with something like dismay, *both inside and out. I've never known another man like him.*

When he sat down again, Adam briefly glanced at Caitlin, then looked away as though uncomfortable. "You're right, you know," he admitted rather reluctantly. "I don't let very many people get close to me. Dane and Felicia are the only ones. At one time I had hopes they'd end up together, but Felicia was all fired up to have a career of her own. As for Dane—you never know what he's thinking."

He stretched out on the sleeping bag once more. "Dane had been at the ranch a few years before I realized he was involved in something besides ranching. I found out he was working with the authorities to help stop the drug smuggling across the border. At the time the whole idea sounded exciting to me, and I insisted on getting in on it."

"Is that what you're doing down here now?" Caitlin forced herself to think about what he was saying and tried to ignore how much the sight of him affected her.

"Yes. However, after two years I've discovered there's more drudgery than excitement, and more danger than I anticipated."

She could certainly understand that after what she had witnessed. "Did those men who tried to kill you know you were with the drug enforcement people?"

"I don't know. I wish I did. I've been working undercover, getting involved with a group of smugglers transporting the drugs. In the process other dealers have been pushed out." His gaze met hers. "Any number of factions could have wanted to get rid of me without even knowing I'm an agent."

Caitlin shivered. "You're lucky to be alive," she said, her gaze drawn hypnotically to the blaze once again.

"Yes. But I wouldn't have made it without you." He studied her profile, which was partially lit by the firelight. "You never told me how you got from Seattle, Washington, to the mountains of Mexico. What made you move?"

"I used to have an aunt who lived in San Antonio. When I was younger, I spent part of my summer vacation with her. She loved the mountains, and we always went to Monterrey whenever I visited." She leaned her head back against the chair and closed her eyes.

"During the months after the accident when I was sure I was going crazy, I would remember the mountains and the peace and serenity I'd always felt whenever I was here."

"There are mountains in the States, you know," he said quietly.

"Yes, I know. I lived near the Cascade Range. But these had become familiar friends. I found myself dreaming about them and began to see myself living in a cabin high in the mountains—away from everything and everyone."

"You escaped from the pressure of your new awareness."

"Yes."

"Caitlin, no one can escape life indefinitely."

"I'm not escaping from life. I have my own life here, and I'm content with it."

"Alone?" His intent gaze met hers, and Caitlin discovered she was having difficulty meeting his eyes.

"I enjoy being alone."

"You feel safer being alone, you mean. There's a difference." Adam slowly came to his feet. He reached down and took her hand from her lap, gently pulling her up to stand in front of him.

Cupping his hands around her face, he tilted her head so that she was looking up at him from only a few inches away. "You've left out one very important ingredient in your life, you know."

Her eyes felt locked to his gaze. She could feel his body aligned against hers and could barely prevent the shiver that tingled down her spine. Caitlin seemed to have lost her power of speech, and she unconsciously ran her tongue across her dry lips.

"What's that?" she managed to ask.

"You've allowed no room in your life for love." Adam closed the distance between them, pulling her closer against him while he did what he'd been wanting to do for days . . . weeks . . . possibly a lifetime.

Adam kissed her. He touched, tasted and explored the wonders she had to offer, moving with careful ease—touching her upper lip with his tongue, softly nibbling on her bottom lip, pulling it into his mouth and at the same time finding entry for his tongue. He took his time, lazily exploring her with his mouth, his hands, his entire body. She felt so good in his arms, better, if possible, than his dreams and imaginings had led him to believe. He wondered how he had ever been able to live with her this long without touching her. He knew in that moment that he never wanted to spend another day that didn't include her in his arms.

Caitlin felt as though she were in shock. During the past several years no one had touched her. She had forgotten how it felt to have someone's arms around her, hugging her. She hadn't known how it would feel to be pressed so closely to the man who had occupied so much of her time and thoughts during the past few weeks.

His kiss seemed to paralyze her, as though by his touch Adam had taken possession of her soul. No one had ever kissed her in the lazy yet very thorough way he was doing, filling her mind and senses with a yearning to be a part of another person, to accept his possession, give in to his silent insistence that the two of them belonged together.

Was he aware of the growing feelings for him that had become a part of her? Did he know what his touch was doing to her?

Sometime during that kiss Caitlin tentatively began to respond. Her tongue met his in a shy greeting, and she slid her arms timidly around his neck in an effort to get closer to him and to enjoy the wondrous sensations that seemed to be bubbling up from within her and flowing throughout her body like expensive champagne.

When her knees gave way, Adam effortlessly lifted her in his arms and knelt in front of the fireplace, placing her on his sleeping bag. Her hood had long since fallen from her head, and while one arm held her close to him, he slipped the robe from her shoulders.

Stretching out to lie beside her, Adam continued to kiss her—soft kisses on her eyes, her cheeks, her nose—then, as though starved for the taste of her, his mouth sought hers once more.

Her voluminous flannel gown demurely buttoned from the waist to the ruffled neckline at the throat.

Because of the tremor in his hand, Adam fumbled with the buttonholes for a moment. When they were opened, he slipped his hand inside her gown and felt the heat of her body against his palm.

Adam wanted her so badly he ached with it. He needed to touch and explore her, to discover everything there was to know about her, to claim her and make her a part of who and what he was, just as he would become a part of her in the same way.

When his hand slid to her breast and encircled it, he felt her body move convulsively.

"It's all right, love," he said in a low, gentle voice. "I want to love you, that's all. Just love you." He leaned down and placed his mouth over the tip of her breast, his tongue playfully nudging the extremely sensitive peak.

Deep-rooted alarms began to jangle within Caitlin. She had always been shy, even with Rick. Despite her engagement, she had never allowed him the freedom Adam was currently enjoying. Caitlin knew that once she gave herself to Adam she would never be the same again. That in the giving of herself to him she would lose a necessary part of her survival abilities—her need to live apart from the world, which included Adam.

She lowered her trembling hands from around his neck so that she could move away from him. Instead, her hands slid to his hair, the soft curls wrapping around her fingers the same way he had managed to wrap himself around her heart.

Adam felt her stiffen, her hands restlessly clutching his head to her breast. Her rapid breathing resulted in a soft panting that he found extremely erotic.

Reluctantly he raised his head and looked down into her face.

Slowly she opened her eyes.

He saw her flushed cheeks and kiss-swollen lips. The expression in her eyes was so vulnerable that it almost brought tears to his.

She saw his eyes burning with desire and a deeper emotion that almost frightened her with its intensity. His mouth was slightly moist from repeated contact with hers.

"I love you, Caitlin."

The words were so soft they scarcely made a ripple in the silence around them; their impact was so profound they could have been shouted.

She lay beside him, dazed with the avalanche of feelings that had almost buried her during the past several moments.

"You can't," she finally managed to say.

His mouth turned up with a quirk of amusement. "And who's going to stop me?"

"But you mustn't."

"Why not?"

"It won't work."

"What won't work?" he asked with amused patience.

"You. Me. Us."

"On the contrary, my love. I think you...me... us...work very well together." He glanced down at his hand where it rested lovingly cupped around her breast. One of his legs lay across both of hers, leaving her in no doubt how much he was affected by her. "There's nothing to be afraid of, you know," he continued. "Loving someone is very normal and natural. I think you'll find it quite enjoyable, once you get used to the idea."

Caitlin closed her eyes, unable to face the warm expression on his face, the loving concern in his eyes.

"I can't, Adam. Don't ask that of me."

"You can't what, little one?"

"Love you." She refused to open her eyes and see how he accepted her statement. She felt him tense slightly, then he shifted, moving his hand and leg so that he was no longer intimately touching her.

"Why not?" he finally asked in the charged silence.

"Surely that's obvious. Our life-styles are not exactly compatible." She turned her head and opened her eyes so that she could watch the fire and not see his face.

"Life-styles have been altered before, you know," he pointed out in a light tone that in no way disguised the seriousness of his remark.

"Somehow I can't see you spending the rest of your life here in the mountains with me."

"And is this where you intend to spend the rest of your life, Caitlin? Here in the mountains?"

"Yes."

The word was stark, to the point, and uttered without hesitation.

"I see," Adam finally said in a low voice.

Did he? Could he possibly see and understand the pain she had escaped from? It had taken her years to accept her difference from other people, to realize that she could find no other place where she would be safe from the stigma of being different.

She had tried to fit in, had honestly tried. After missing months of school she had returned to college, only to discover how different the world was when another person's thoughts and desires were known to her and when she learned how seldom a person said what he thought or believed. She discovered how little people respected truth.

Caitlin knew that Adam wanted to make love to her. She didn't need her psychic abilities to gain that information. She even knew that he was sincere in expressing what he felt for her.

For now. Once he returned to his real life, he'd realize how out of place she would be. She didn't belong in his world. She never would.

Adam sat up, leaning his elbows on his bent knees, his head in his hands. His head pounded with the sexual excitement that pumped through his body.

"Your head hurts," Caitlin said, feeling his physical and emotional pain as though it were her own.

"Among other things," he acknowledged wryly.

She got up, slipped her robe back onto her shoulders and went to the stove. The water was still hot. She quickly made him a drink from the herbs that would ease his pain. Bringing it back to him, she silently handed him the cup.

He looked at it in surprise. His mind had been filled with a whirlwind of thoughts, explanations, ideas, arguments. And pain. The pain seemed to wash over all the rest, coloring them, expanding them, overwhelming them.

Without thinking, he took a sip of the hot liquid, belatedly remembering the bitter taste of the drink.

Somehow the taste fit his mood, and he quickly drained the contents, then stood up.

"I'll bring in more wood. You'd better try to get some sleep." He didn't look at her. Caitlin could feel his need to get away from her, away from the cloying confines of the cabin. Without saying a word, she walked over, took off her robe and crawled into bed. She watched Adam walk out into the night, his coat collar turned up against the cold. He closed the door quietly behind him.

She hadn't wanted to hurt him. But wasn't it better to face reality now rather than wait until the unsuitability of a relationship between them became as obvious to him as it was to her?

Caitlin curled up on her side, with her back to the door. There was no exact measurement for pain, she decided, drifting off to sleep. It was just there, trapping the unwary with its sudden needle-sharp presence.

Five

———

Caitlin woke up the next morning to the scent of freshly brewed coffee. Pushing her hair away from her face, she realized she had overslept. Adam had drawn the curtain that shielded the bed from the rest of the room, leaving that corner in shadows.

She must have gone to sleep almost immediately after returning to bed. She never heard Adam come back into the cabin.

As soon as she was dressed, Caitlin slid the curtain back, unsurprised to discover herself alone in the cabin. She was always so aware of Adam that she knew she would have felt his presence had he been there.

Opening the door, she looked around the clearing. It was empty. She felt almost disoriented. This was the first morning since Adam had been at the cabin that she had slept longer than he had. Her morning routine seemed fuzzy in her head, and she wasn't sure what to do first.

Caitlin wandered into the lean-to and found Adam milking the goat.

"You have talents I never suspected," she said with a smile, trying to lighten the atmosphere between them.

He had filled the pail and was setting it aside when she spoke. He glanced up at her, then looked away, but not before she saw the expression in his eyes. Their gray-green depths spoke of love and hurt, passion and pain. He hadn't succeeded in putting the night behind him any better than she had.

"I thought you could use some help this morning," he responded, his tone even. Getting up from the small stool, he leaned over, picked up the pail of milk and handed it to her.

"You didn't have to do that."

"I know. But you needed your rest."

"How long have you been awake?"

"I don't know. Does it matter?" He started back toward the cabin. Without looking at her, he said, "I'm leaving today."

She'd known that from the moment she had opened her eyes. She just hadn't wanted to face it.

"Can you tell me how to get to the village from here?"

"I'll show you."

"That really isn't necessary."

How polite they had become with each other.

"I'm afraid it is. I don't think you would find it otherwise. The path isn't defined. I use several animal trails to get there. You would have to know when to leave one and look for another." She went into the cabin and put the milk away. "I'll get breakfast ready and prepare something to eat along the way."

"How long does it take to get there?"

"About two hours, depending on the pace."

There didn't seem to be much else to say. Caitlin returned his pistol and holster to him. He checked it over, then put it on without comment. They moved carefully around each other, consciously refraining from touching, as though by keeping a proper distance they could maintain the polite fiction they had adopted of being merely acquaintances and nothing more.

Breakfast passed in silence, and within the hour Adam and Caitlin were hiking down the trail toward the village.

She set an easy pace, unobtrusively making certain that he didn't tire, pointing out areas of interest as they went along. He listened without comment, observing everything around them.

By the time they reached the village, Adam knew he'd pushed himself and was disgusted at the signs of weakness. His body had never let him down before, but he knew he was running on nerves and sheer willpower. There was no point in delaying his return to the real world, as he thought of it. And there was a definite danger in staying. He loved Caitlin, and continuing to share the small cabin with her without making love to her was a torture he didn't intend to continue.

They walked through the main street of the village, with Caitlin pointing out the shops, and ended up at a small taverna where they ordered something to drink while Adam talked to the owner.

A few people recognized him from their visits to see Caitlin, and they surprised him by greeting him with shy smiles. He could see why Caitlin had grown attached to these people.

Right now he had to keep his mind on his priorities. He needed transportation north. Without money or identification, transportation might prove difficult.

His conversation with the owner of the taverna didn't improve his mood any.

"What's wrong?" Caitlin asked when he returned to the table where she waited.

"I hadn't realized how remote we are. There's very little traffic through the village. I'm going to have to stick around and take my chances on getting out of here."

Caitlin could see the lines of strain around his eyes and the dark smudges beneath them that betrayed his lack of sleep from the night before. She felt the dull throb of pain in his head. This was too soon for him to be so active, but she knew she couldn't ask him to stay any longer. For both their sakes, he had to go.

They left the taverna, and Caitlin went to one of the small shops where she bought a few supplies. Conversation had become more and more difficult between them. And why not? There was nothing to add to what had already been said the night before.

Eventually Caitlin faced the fact that there was nothing more for her to do in the village. She glanced around at the empty street, then at Adam. "I really need to start back. It will be dark soon."

"Yes."

Hesitantly she placed her hand on the sleeve of his coat. "Take care of yourself." She watched a small muscle leap in his jaw and knew he was finding their leave-taking as difficult as she was.

"You, too."

They stood there for a moment in silence, then Caitlin said, "Well—goodbye, Adam. God bless."

She turned and walked away from him, forcing herself not to glance over her shoulder.

Caitlin had taken three or four steps when she heard Adam's voice.

"Wait!" She turned around and found him striding toward her. "I'll be damned if I'm going to tell you goodbye in the middle of some godforsaken Mexican settlement with everyone looking on." He took her firmly by the elbow and began to walk beside her. "Since it doesn't look as though I'll be leaving here for a while, I can go partway with you."

Caitlin could feel her heart pounding painfully in her chest. This was much harder than she could handle without breaking down, but she had no choice.

"Are you going to be okay?" he asked when she remained silent.

She nodded without looking at him.

"Aren't you even going to talk to me?"

Looking straight ahead, she said, "What do you want me to say?"

"How about 'I'm going to miss you, Adam'?"

"That goes without saying."

"No, it doesn't. I want to hear it."

She stopped. They were above the settlement now, out of sight of any signs of civilization. The western sun bathed him in a golden glow of gilt. She would never forget the way he looked at that moment, not as long as she lived. She forced herself to meet his gaze, her eyes filling with tears despite her best intentions.

"I'm going to miss you, Adam," she managed to say past the lump that had formed in her throat.

With slow, deliberate movements, he slipped his arms around her, pulling her close to him. "I'm going to miss you, too, darlin'. More important, I'm going to miss my heart, since it's staying here in the mountains with you. I'm not sure how well I'm going to be able to function without it."

Caitlin rested her head against his chest. Her tears finally overflowed and slowly trickled down her cheeks.

"Oh, Adam" was all she could say.

With his forefinger under her chin, Adam tilted her head so that his mouth found hers. His possession seemed perfectly natural to both of them, familiar because she was such a part of him. Adam didn't know how he was going to walk away from her. She had become as necessary to him as the air that filled his lungs and gave him life. He loved her. How could he possibly leave her?

Caitlin felt as though she no longer had a will of her own. As soon as Adam touched her, she became pliant in his arms. Her response to his kiss left no doubt in either one's mind that she shared his feelings.

They stood there in the mountain wilderness, clinging to each other, devastated by the impending loss they faced.

The whine of a bullet and the cracking sound of the discharge came simultaneously, and Adam reacted automatically. He pushed Caitlin toward the ground, shoving her behind a boulder alongside the trail. Another shot was fired, and pieces of the rock ricocheted around them.

"Are you all right?" he whispered, touching Caitlin on the shoulder. Not looking at him, she nodded without speaking.

The sudden unexpected attack left them both stunned. Violence had no business in the peaceful mountains, and yet it had found them.

"I've got to see who this is. Stay here and don't move, okay?" Once again she nodded.

Adam's gun was already in his hand, and he crept farther away from the trail, circling the area where the gunshots had been fired. He kept the brush, boulders and trees between him and his would-be assailant, moving as rapidly as possible on silent feet.

It hadn't occurred to Adam that someone was still out to kill him. How had they traced him to the village? He wondered how long they had been waiting for him to appear. Like some amateur, he'd walked right into their hands without suspecting anything, making no attempt to cover his tracks.

Because of his carelessness he'd managed to involve Caitlin. Damn. He couldn't leave her alone now. The picture had changed. She would have to go with him. Adam silently cursed again. How could he have done this to her?

A cold fury swept over him. He would find out who this was and get to the bottom of the situation.

The woods were silent. The gunman had stopped firing. Adam paused, torn between going after him and getting Caitlin away from there. He couldn't take any chances with her life. Hesitating for only a moment, he made his decision and turned back to where he'd left Caitlin waiting.

She hadn't moved but sat huddled, her head resting on her drawn-up knees. He knelt down beside her. "I've lost him for the moment," he whispered. "He's probably watching the trail we were on, waiting for us to reappear. There's no telling who he is. He could have been sitting there in the taverna for all I know."

Caitlin raised her head, her face totally without color. Slowly she shook her head. "No, he wasn't. I would have noticed him." She paused, as though gathering her thoughts. "He's the same man who drove the car that forced you off the road."

Adam studied her intently, not liking the look of her eyes. She was going into shock, which wasn't surprising. Not many people were used to being shot at. "Are you sure?"

"Reasonably."

"Damn! I wish I could see him...know who I'm looking for."

He stood, taking her arm and pulling her up, too. She winced and moved away from him. "Look, Adam. I'll go on back to the cabin. Maybe if you return to the village, someone will be able to point him out to you. After all, everyone there would know when there's a stranger in town. I should have thought to ask."

"I wasn't thinking very clearly myself today." All of his thoughts had been on the pain of leaving Caitlin behind. His lack of clear thinking had almost gotten them killed.

She tried to move away from him, but he still held her arm. "I don't want you continuing on that path." He guided her behind the rocks for some distance until he spotted a trail he had seen earlier. "Follow that until you get over the ridge. I'll be along shortly."

"No." She met his gaze squarely.

"What do you mean, no?"

"There's no reason for you to come back to the cabin. You need to stay at the village. I'll be okay."

He stared at her for a moment in silence. She was upset, and he supposed she had every reason to be. Adam saw no point in standing there debating the issue. He would see what he could find, then return to the cabin.

Without commenting on her statement, he leaned over and gently kissed her, then watched as she turned away and began to follow the path. He waited until she had disappeared from view before he started down once more.

He didn't like the shocked state Caitlin was in. Her color was pasty white, her eyes dilated, her breathing labored. He couldn't leave her alone after what she'd gone through today.

But if he could find the gunman first, that would be a relief to both of them.

After thoroughly searching the area, Adam found nothing but some shell casings. Whoever he was, he must have decided to withdraw and wait for another time.

Adam silently thanked him for the warning. He would be better prepared next time.

He started back up the trail toward the cabin and Caitlin. Adam had to know that she was all right. He reached the place where the gunman had fired at them and stepped off the path, intending to follow the same route she had in case he could catch up with her before she reached home.

Glancing down, he caught sight of color, brilliant and damp. He bent closer to examine what looked to be blood. With a gnawing feeling in the pit of his stomach, he touched one of the small drops and confirmed his suspicion.

As he followed the trail of blood that led into the mountains, a helpless anger wrapped itself around him.

She'd been hit. And she hadn't even told him.

Damn her! Why hadn't she said something? He should have known that her shocked condition was more than just being scared. She was too strong for that. He remembered that she'd kept her arms across her chest, her hands tightly gripping her shoulders.

Her shoulder! Of course. He hadn't seen it because he hadn't been looking for it. His mind had been on the gunman. She hadn't made a sound when she was hit. He shook his head. He wasn't sure at the moment what he would do when he found her, hug her or murder her himself!

But first he had to find her.

She had made considerable progress along the trail. He'd almost decided she'd gotten all the way back to the cabin when he saw her. She probably would have made it if she hadn't stopped to rest.

She sat next to a large tree, her body braced against it, her head back and her eyes closed. Her hand still clutched her shoulder, but now the blood had soaked through her heavy hand-woven shirt, covering her fingers and slowly dripping down her arm.

When Adam reached out to touch her, he absently noted that his hand was shaking, which surprised him. An icy calm had seemed to settle over him as soon as he saw her.

"Let me see," he said, his voice gruff.

Her head came up in a convulsive jerk, her eyes flying open. Her pale skin looked transparent. "What are you doing here?"

He knelt beside her, gently removing her hand from her shoulder and ignoring her question. "Why didn't you tell me you were hurt, dammit," he said through gritted teeth. "How bad is it?"

Wearily she rested her head against the tree once more. "I'm all right, Adam. It's just a flesh wound. By the time I get some medication on it, I'll be fine. There was no reason for you to come back."

"That's a matter of opinion. If I hadn't been worried and decided to check on how you were, you could have been passed out along the trail somewhere."

"No. I just needed to rest a few moments, that's all."

He lifted her shirt away, exposing her shoulder. The bullet had grazed her upper shoulder, leaving a jagged tear in her flesh.

"It's not all that bad," she insisted.

"Bad enough," he replied, getting to his feet. He picked her up and started toward the cabin.

"Adam, don't carry me. You're in no condition to—"

"If you know what's good for you, you won't say another word," he said through clenched jaws. "Not one...more...word."

Caitlin hurt too badly to talk. Every step she'd taken jolted and jarred her until she had almost cried out with the pain. She had seen too many wounds not to understand that hers was not serious. But she couldn't deny that it hurt.

Wearily she leaned her head on Adam's shoulder, too tired to argue. He was there, regardless of what she could say. He was also very angry with her. Caitlin had never seen Adam angry before. She wasn't sure she ever wanted to see him angry again.

That was the last thing she remembered thinking.

By the time Adam reached the clearing, he realized that Caitlin was either asleep or unconscious. Either one was a blessing at the moment. There was barely enough light to find his way across the clearing. He shoved the cabin door open with his foot and felt his way over to the bed.

The room was cold, since they had put out the fire before leaving that morning. Adam lit the lamp, covered Caitlin with a blanket and built a fire that quickly took the chill from the room.

He pumped some water into a bowl and made preparations to clean her wound. Quickly undressing her, he left only her panties on since her bra was in the way of the area where he needed to work. He covered her with a blanket, leaving the wounded area exposed.

"How are you feeling?" he asked in a neutral tone, while he bathed and cleaned the wounded area.

"All right," she whispered.

The weakness in her voice filled him with pain. "Of course you are," he said through gritted teeth. The jagged wound in her delicate skin caused him to curse silently to himself. She didn't deserve this. Caitlin of all people had no use for violence. She was a healer— a gentle, caring person who had no business being mixed up with him and what he was doing.

He poured a cup of water for her and, after gently lifting her head, held the cup to her lips. She drank from the cup, then laid her head back against the pillow with a sigh.

There was no sense letting her know how upset he was. Brushing her hair away from her brow, he tried to smile, but since he was still concerned over her pallor, his lips barely moved.

"We've reversed our roles, I guess," she said in response to his smile.

"Looks that way."

"Adam, please don't feel you have to stay here with me. I know you need to get back to Monterrey."

"Dammit, Caitlin, don't you understand that things have changed now? Whoever is after me not only knows I'm not dead, but also knows approximately where they can find me and that I'm with you. I can't go off and leave you unprotected."

"They don't want me. Even if they managed to find this cabin—which I doubt very much—once they discovered you were gone, they'd have no further interest in me."

"A nice thought to hold." He got up and added more firewood onto the fire. Without turning around he said, "Do you want something to eat?"

"Not particularly."

NOW THAT THE DOOR IS OPEN . . .
Peel off the bouquet and send it on the postpaid order card to receive:

4 FREE BOOKS
from

Silhouette ❤ *Desire*®

An attractive burgundy umbrella FREE! And a mystery gift as an EXTRA BONUS!

PLUS

MONEY-SAVING HOME DELIVERY!

Once you receive your 4 FREE books and gifts, you'll be able to open your door to more great romance reading month after month. Enjoy the convenience of previewing 6 brand-new books every month delivered right to your home months before they appear in stores. Each book is yours for only $2.24—.26¢ less than the retail price, with no additional charges for home delivery.

SPECIAL EXTRAS—FREE!

You'll also receive the Silhouette Books Newsletter FREE with every book shipment. Every issue is filled with interviews, news about upcoming books and more! And as a valued reader, we'll be sending you additional free gifts from time to time—as a token of our appreciation.

NO-RISK GUARANTEE!

— There's no obligation to buy—and the free books and gifts are yours to keep forever.
— You pay the lowest price possible and receive books months before they appear in stores.
— You may end your subscription anytime—just write and let us know.

RETURN THE POSTPAID ORDER CARD TODAY AND OPEN YOUR DOOR TO THESE 4 EXCITING LOVE-FILLED NOVELS. THEY ARE YOURS ABSOLUTELY FREE ALONG WITH YOUR FOLDING UMBRELLA AND MYSTERY GIFT.

"I think I'll heat up some soup. Maybe you'll feel like eating some by the time I have it ready."

He knew he was not hiding his fear and frustration very well, but he couldn't seem to help it. He couldn't remember ever having been quite so scared. The realization that Caitlin was hurt had frightened him even more than the knowledge that his car was being forced off the road.

The relief he'd felt at seeing the flesh wound had been transmitted as anger. Determined to get a grip on his emotions, he found a pan and began to heat the soup.

Caitlin was asleep by the time it was ready, and he decided that rest was the best thing for her.

Adam ate, then paced the floor, trying to decide what to do. Periodically he checked the bandage he'd placed on her shoulder. There was no sign of bleeding. He knew her arm and shoulder would be stiff and sore by morning, but hopefully there would be no infection.

Remembering how effective the drink was for relieving pain, Adam made up some of the tea she had given to him. He almost laughed at the sleepy face she made as she drank it. Served her right. However, the brew worked, and that was the important thing. She would be able to rest more comfortably now.

When he realized there was nothing further he could do, he went outside and fed the animals, including Chula, who had followed him into the lean-to and nosed into his hip pocket, looking for something to eat. Adam returned to the cabin and checked on Caitlin. She hadn't stirred.

Now that the adrenaline had stopped flowing
through him, Adam realized how tired he was. After
little or no sleep the night before, he'd put in a physically exhausting day, not to mention the wear and tear
on his emotions. He was more than ready to get some
rest himself.

The bedroll was lying against the wall where he'd
left it that morning. He glanced over his shoulder at
Caitlin. Would he hear her if she stirred and needed
something? He knew she'd never ask him for help; she
was so damned independent.

Of course, if he were to sleep on the other half of the
bed, she couldn't move without his being aware of it.
What a thin excuse to justify something he wanted to
do, he reflected. If it was up to him, he would spend
every night for the rest of his life in her bed. He wondered if he'd ever convince her that the idea held
considerable merit.

Quietly Adam undressed and crawled into bed next
to her. He could feel the tight muscles in his body relax, and he sighed with relief. He'd certainly earned
the right to a good night's rest.

Caitlin stirred restlessly beside him, and he shifted
toward her. Leaning on his elbow, Adam looked down
at her. She seemed to be dreaming, muttering something, restlessly shifting her head and arms. He was
afraid she was going to jar her shoulder, but he wasn't
sure what he could do to help.

Hesitantly he brushed her hair from her forehead.
The touch of his hand seemed to soothe her, and she
quietened. He moved closer and murmured comfort-
ingly. The slight frown line between her brow disappeared, and she relaxed against him.

Adam drifted off to sleep with his arm draped across her, his hand tangled in her hair.

Caitlin was so thirsty. Her throat hurt whenever she tried to swallow. And her shoulder felt as though a branding iron was being held against it, searing the flesh. She whimpered, the noise bringing her fully awake and aware of her surroundings.

The first thing she noticed was that Adam was beside her in bed, sleeping heavily. The second thing she noticed was that he had an arm and a leg thrown over her, effectively stopping her from moving.

She felt so vulnerable tucked away in his arms, particularly since neither one of them had on much in the way of clothing. She wore a pair of panties, and he'd dispensed with everything but his briefs.

The nights she had slept beside him had been nothing like this. Now they were sleeping like lovers.

Lovers. Wasn't that what they were in every sense— except for the physical expression of that love? In the quiet hours of the night, Caitlin faced the depth of their feelings for each other.

She probably would have fallen for Adam, regardless of the circumstances that brought them together, but caring for him when he was so vulnerable had made an indelible impression on her. She was also aware of his feelings for her. They were equally intense. He hadn't needed to explain them. She knew.

However, not even for the love she felt for him and he felt for her could she leave the retreat that had given her back her sanity. Their love had been given an opportunity to develop and expand in a carefully controlled environment. In the outside world, their love could easily shrivel and disappear through no fault of theirs.

Adam had only been with her in her own surroundings. He didn't know how upset she became around people who seemed to crowd in on her from all directions. And there was no way she could explain her feelings to him so that he would understand.

No one seemed to fully understand the trauma she experienced. She had to deal with it in the best way she knew how. Living in the mountains was her solution.

Perhaps Adam could come back to visit her from time to time. She smiled at the possible positive solution. Just knowing he was a part of her life, however distant, would be a comfort to her.

The throbbing pain in her shoulder drew her attention away from her thoughts, and she shifted restlessly, trying to ease the discomfort.

Adam woke up immediately.

"Are you all right, darlin'?" he mumbled, his words slurred with sleep. His hand shifted so that it lay across her breast. He stiffened and hastily removed his arm and leg from her.

"I'm a little thirsty, that's all," she said in a whisper, her voice nonexistent.

He sat up. "I'll get you some more of that ghastly brew. It should help the pain, as well as quench your thirst. In fact, you may never want anything else to drink after that." He got out of bed and strode over to the cabinet. While waiting for the water to heat, he wandered back over to her.

"I hope you don't mind my sharing the bed with you. I was afraid I wouldn't hear you if you needed anything."

"I don't mind," she said quietly, although she didn't look at him.

He went back and made her drink. When she sat up, she remembered her state of undress. "Would you mind handing me my robe?" she asked with as much dignity as she could muster.

"Why? Do you need to get up?"

"No. I don't have any clothes on."

"Oh." He draped a soft woolen shawl over her shoulders. "There. That should keep the chill off you."

Since she held the cup in both of her hands, she had no recourse but to sit quietly while he arranged the folds of the shawl to suit his purposes, his knuckles continuing to brush provocatively against her bare breasts.

Her breathing quickened, and Adam knew she was no more immune to what they shared than he was. He crawled back into bed carefully so that she wouldn't spill her drink. Stretching out beside her, he lay there enjoying the intimate view of her profile so close to him.

"Surely you can see that I can't leave you here now," he said in a reasonable tone. "As soon as you're feeling well enough to travel, I'll take you home with me."

His calm determination unsettled her, but she refused to allow him to see her reaction to his statement. "Nothing has changed, Adam. I'm not leaving here."

"The hell it hasn't!" he exclaimed, forgetting his promise to himself to stay calm and quiet. "There's someone out there who tried to kill you!"

"Not me. No one was shooting at me. I just got in the way."

"If you think I find that statement comforting, you're wrong. You can't stay here, Caitlin. That's all there is to it."

"It isn't your choice to make, Adam." Her voice from the shadows sounded very firm and filled with conviction.

But he had to try to get her to see reason. "How are you going to take care of yourself?"

"The same way I always have. My shoulder is going to be a little stiff and sore for a few days, but I'm all right." Her voice was beginning to sound drowsy, and he knew the tea was working its magic on her.

He took the cup and helped her slide back down into the covers. "I love you so damned much," he muttered in frustration.

"You can always come back to visit me, you know."

"You can be certain I'm going to do that! I haven't given up on us. Not by a long shot. But I've got to get back to the States and let everyone know I'm still alive and that someone is trying their best to remedy that situation."

She turned over so that she was facing him. "Be careful, please. You are so special, Adam. I don't want anything to happen to you." She placed her hand along his jawline, feeling the tightness that signaled the control he was keeping over himself.

"Caitlin, love," he said, having to try one more time. "Please come home with me."

"No."

How could he argue with her anymore? No matter what he said, the fact remained that he couldn't force her to do something she refused to do. He'd often thought his sister to be the most stubborn person he'd ever known. Caitlin could give Felicia lessons, heaven forbid.

Her hand slipped from his jaw, and he knew she was asleep.

There was nothing more he could do or say. As much as he wanted to remain in their own little Utopia, Adam knew too much depended on his getting back. Whatever he had accidentally stumbled across in his investigation was too serious for him to lose any more time reporting it.

He knew she would resent his interference, but he intended to contact Antonio's family in the village and have them check on her. Adam had to be sure she was all right and that she didn't suffer because of her own stubbornness.

Pulling Caitlin closer into the circle of his arms, he closed his eyes, enjoying her sweet scent, the warmth of her body, the soft sounds of her breathing. He would have to learn to live without her for a while. He refused to accept that he had to give her up permanently.

Six

Adam's dream seemed to remove him from his present situation, transporting him to a happier time. He was at the ranch, riding in from one of the pastures when he saw Caitlin, waving to him from the bluffs near the river. Her hair was loose, and the wind teased it, causing the curls to dance around her face. He guided his horse away from the homeward trail and allowed his mount to pick its way down the slope, cross the river at the shallow rapids and find the trail that led to the top of the bluffs where Caitlin waited.

In his dream he recognized his relief at seeing her. She'd been gone from his life for so long, but now she was there, waiting for him.

The waiting was over.

Adam slid from the saddle and swooped her up in his arms, twirling her around while his lips covered hers.

Adam's dream dissolved slowly, and he realized that he was holding Caitlin in his arms and kissing her. His breathing sounded harsh in the quiet room. He was holding her as though he never intended to let her go, and when he forced himself to relax his hold on her, he discovered he was shaking.

Caitlin was curled up in his arms with her arms around his waist, her legs entwined with his, her injured shoulder ignored. Her lips were moist and slightly swollen from his kisses, and it was all he could do not to continue.

Her eyelashes slowly fluttered open. "Adam?" she murmured uncertainly.

"Yes?"

"Were you kissing me just now, or was I dreaming?"

"A little of both, I'm afraid. I think we've both been dreaming."

She stretched and sighed, and he realized with a lopsided smile that she was still asleep. Otherwise she would not be so unconcerned with their sleeping position.

And when she pulled his head down toward hers once more, he could no more resist her than he could stop breathing. Her mouth searched for his, and with a sigh of pleasure, she began to kiss him once more.

He returned her kiss, loving the feel of her in his arms, enjoying the sensations that no other woman had ever been able to create within him.

Adam realized that if they didn't stop now there would be no turning back. He also knew that he could not make love to her tonight and walk away from her tomorrow.

He pulled away slightly, kissing her lightly on her eyelids, her nose and her cheeks. She smiled. "You probably won't even remember this in the morning, and it's just as well," he whispered. "I know you love me. Your every action fairly shouts your feelings." He traced the slight arch of her eyebrow with his finger. "I'll be back. Even if I have to go through hell first, I'll be back," he vowed, as much to himself as to her. "I'll never be without you in my life, regardless of what it takes to keep you close to me."

When Caitlin woke up, bright sunlight flooded the room. She was alone in the cabin and was reminded of the morning before. Adam was probably outside taking care of the animals for her.

Her shoulder felt much better today. She knew it was healing. She'd slept so well the night before, no doubt partly due to the potent tea Adam had made up for her. The tea was probably responsible for some of her dreams, as well. She smiled at her memories. It was just as well that Adam didn't know what had transpired in some of them.

It took her a while to pull on her clothes and yet Adam still hadn't returned by the time she was dressed. Caitlin decided to go outside looking for him. When she reached the lean-to she discovered that the animals had all been fed but Adam was nowhere around. Puzzled, she returned to the cabin. Only then did she notice that he hadn't made coffee, which was unusual. Caitlin walked over to the counter and for the first time saw his note propped against the coffeepot.

Please forgive me for not waking you to say goodbye. We said that yesterday, and I wasn't sure I could leave you today if I didn't get away now. I have no choice at the moment but to go, but I'll be back as soon as I can. You and I have some unfinished business.

> Don't forget me.
> Adam

Caitlin stared at the note for a long time, trying not to face the fact that she wasn't going to see him again. Of course he had done what he had to do. There was no reason for him to linger. He knew she was going to be all right.

She kept reading the last line over and over. *Don't forget me.*

How could she possibly forget him? He'd said he would come back, and she believed him. In the meantime, she had her life to live—the life she had chosen.

Caitlin became aware of the ache in her shoulder. She carefully folded Adam's note and placed it in one of her books, returning the book to the shelf.

A part of her life was finished now, but she felt richer because of what she had experienced.

She had learned about love, its pain as well as its beauty. Perhaps one couldn't exist without the other.

Adam's entry into the village was considerably different from the day before. After making sure no one was in sight, he slipped into the taverna by the rear entrance. He waited until the owner was alone, then signaled to him. The man looked at him in surprise.

"Someone shot at me yesterday while I was up in the hills. Did you hear anything?"

The man's eyes widened. "No, *señor*. I heard nothing."

"Have any strangers come into town recently?"

"You, *señor*."

"Besides me."

The man thought for a moment. "No."

"Are you sure? Think about it. Anyone at all."

"Well-l-l-l." The man scratched his head. "Alfredo Cortez, he's lived here a few weeks—I don't know exactly for how long—"

"You mean, since February?"

"Oh, yes. I'd say since then...possibly."

"What is he doing here? Visiting with family, working?"

"I don't know. He comes in here every afternoon—sits around and visits."

"Do you ever hear him ask questions?"

"Like you are?"

"Yes, like I am. Does he ever say why he's here, like maybe because he's looking for someone?"

"Maybe...maybe not. He doesn't bother anybody, you know."

Adam felt the frustration of being the outsider. Obviously this Cortez had managed to mingle with the locals successfully. Adam realized that with his blond coloring and American heritage he was easily identifiable. He didn't dare hang around the village waiting for a ride in the event that Cortez was the man looking for him.

"Thanks for your help. I really appreciate it," Adam said to the owner. He wished he had some money on him. He might have learned more if he could have encouraged the man, but there was no sense in pushing his luck.

Adam slipped out of the taverna without seeing anyone and stood for a few moments in the shelter of the building. He would find Antonio's home and explain about Caitlin's injury. He knew how much the villagers cared for her. She would probably be safer with them than if he stayed to look after her.

Avoiding the main street, Adam eventually found the small house Caitlin had pointed out to him the day before. It didn't take him long to explain, and by the time he left, Adam knew Caitlin would be hovered over by her protective friends. He grinned, thinking of her reaction to their concern. Caitlin probably wouldn't be pleased. She really insisted on being independent.

Hours later Adam was several miles from the village, headed north. He had decided against going into Monterrey. Without any way to identify himself, he was in danger of being picked up as a vagrant, with no chance to prove who he was. During the long walk away from the village he decided to stay as invisible as possible and get to the border. He'd worry about getting across once he got there.

That night he curled up under some brush and tried to sleep. By morning the sky had opened up, and heavy rains fell. For the next several days Adam walked, hitched rides, slept in lean-tos when he could find them, and continued his way north with dogged determination.

Eventually his body rebelled against the abuse he was heaping on himself. He picked up a cough, and his chest hurt. By the time he made it to the border, he was almost too weak to stand.

Adam didn't care. He had made it without getting picked up by the authorities. The next hurdle was to cross into the States.

Getting across the Rio Grande took three days. He spent most of that time in the border patrol office trying to convince them he was who he said he was.

Adam didn't feel as though he'd slept more than an hour or two at a time since he'd left Caitlin, and he couldn't remember the last time he'd eaten. Eventually he was allowed to get in touch with his superiors in San Antonio who confirmed what he had already suspected: he'd been reported missing, presumed dead.

He was very pleased to inform them that he was still around. His next call was to Dane. He was more than a little surprised when Felicia answered.

"What are you doing at the ranch?" he asked when she answered.

"Adam? Is that you? Is that really you? Where are you?"

He laughed, the relief of knowing the worst of his trek was behind him making him feel light-headed.

He told her, and he asked to speak to Dane, giving him the particulars of where he was and that he needed a ride home.

A couple of Agency men showed up, and he was able to give them as full a report as possible. He discovered that the man he had been gathering evidence on had been arrested and that a successful conclusion to the case seemed to be assured.

No one was sure who was behind the attempts on Adam's life. At this point it was anybody's guess.

By the time Dane and Felicia arrived, Adam's store of energy was gone. He slept all the way back to the ranch and did little more than sleep and eat for almost a week afterward. His body finally demanded some care after the punishment it had received.

Adam discovered that his disappearance had caused one good thing to happen: Dane and Felicia had gotten married during the time they had spent looking for him. In addition, they were expecting a baby in late fall.

So Caitlin had been right about them.

Caitlin. She was never out of his thoughts. For many days and nights his memories of her were what had kept him going. He thought about the way she looked, the way she felt in his arms, the way she responded to his kisses.

God! He missed her so. He hadn't been teasing when he told her he'd left part of himself there in the mountains. He wouldn't be whole again until he returned.

In the meantime... he bought a car to replace the one that ended up over the side of the mountain and drove to San Antonio. Robert McFarlane, the head of the regional office, had called a private meeting with him.

Robert chose one of the hotels down along the banks of the San Antonio River. It was a beautiful day, and they sat at one of the many outdoor tables to admire the view and soak up the late-spring sun.

Conversation was casual until after the waitress brought their coffee and left.

Adam filled Rob in on everything that had happened since their last meeting. Then he had some questions of his own.

"Was the man I was supposed to meet ever contacted?" Adam asked.

"Yes. Zeke Taylor managed to contact him not long after you disappeared."

"That makes sense. Zeke's the only other agent who knew about the contact. How did it go?"

"The man gave Zeke all the details—place of exchange, names, the whole thing—so we were able to nail Santiago and make it stick. Unfortunately we never got a chance to thank our informant."

"What do you mean?"

"He was killed within hours after Zeke left him."

"By whom?"

"We haven't found out. We may never find out."

They sat for a while in silence, watching people strolling along the River Walk, enjoying the view.

"Does Zeke know I'm back?"

"Sure. The whole Agency knows. You were the one that came back from the grave."

"I bet he's pleased we managed to finalize this one."

"We all are. This has been one hell of a hard case to crack."

"Do you think the informant's death ties in with the attempt on me?"

"Who can say? It would be a help if you knew what your assailant looks like. Then we could start a manhunt."

"I know. I've thought of that more than once, believe me. There is somebody who's seen him. Unfortunately, she—"

"You mean there's a woman who can finger the guy?"

"Well, yes, except that—"

"What are you waiting for? Bring her in. Show her the mug shots, get her to identify him. Why didn't you say something earlier? Your report stated that you had not seen the men in the car or the gunman near the village."

"I know."

"God! This may be the break we're looking for."

"If I can get her to come."

"What do you mean?"

"Well, the witness lives in the mountains of Mexico—"

"Oh, so she doesn't speak English. Well, that's no problem. We're all bilingual around here."

"She's from Seattle, Washington, and speaks English just fine."

"Oh! Well, then, what's the problem?"

"She won't leave the mountains."

"We're not asking her to move! She'd just visit the office, look at the mug shots, see if she recognizes anyone. You're sure she got a clear look at the guy?"

"Yes."

"Good. When can you get her up here?"

"Good question. I was thinking about taking her to the ranch first."

Rob studied the younger man for a moment in silence. "The ranch, huh? Something tells me there's more than Agency business involved here."

"Maybe."

"Is this the woman who found you and nursed you back to health?"

"Yes."

"Could you be mistaking gratitude for something else?"

"What I feel for Caitlin is a hell of a lot stronger than gratitude, Rob. I have no problem understanding the difference."

Rob laughed. "How the mighty are fallen. I never thought I'd see the day that Adam St. Clair joined the lovesick corps."

Adam grinned ruefully. "Go ahead, rub it in. After all, you being the boss means I can't retaliate."

"Tell me another one. My being the boss has never slowed you down in the past."

"True," Adam agreed complacently.

"I want to see the woman here in the office no later than two weeks from now. That's the most time I can allow on this one. We've got to get some answers and tie up the loose ends. After all, it's your neck they're after. We need to know if your cover's been blown before we can use you down there again. Surely she'll want to cooperate to help keep you around."

"I can only hope."

"I have faith in your persuasive powers, St. Clair," Rob said, standing up. The meeting was now over, and Adam had his orders.

Summer weather came early to the mountains. Caitlin welcomed the opportunity to open her door and windows to the warm air. Her flower garden burst forth with riotous colors, as though to help lift her spirits.

The weeks following Adam's departure had been extremely hard for her. She felt bereft. The cabin was no longer her haven. Instead it was a daily reminder of his presence in her life. Everywhere she looked, she saw him—in front of the fireplace, in her bed, at the table, even milking her goat. Caitlin tried to stay busy, too busy to think about a future that didn't include Adam.

She spent more of her time at the village, helping with the newborn babies, visiting with the mothers and listening to the rambling tales of the old ones.

The villagers insisted on teasing her about her handsome *novio*, even though she insisted he was not her sweetheart or fiancé. They thought they knew better. After all, hadn't they seen the way he looked at her, the way he treated her when they had been together at the village? There were no words that could refute what the villagers had seen with their own eyes.

Caitlin accepted their kindly teasing, knowing it would do no good to continue to protest. Once they saw that Adam would not be returning anytime soon, if at all, the villagers would eventually ease up on the subject.

Late one afternoon in May, Caitlin entered the clearing where the little cabin stood. She was weary, not only physically, since she had gotten little sleep the night before, but emotionally, because she had been sitting beside the bed of a woman old in years, but young in heart. A woman whose death left a definite hole in the lives of those who loved her.

And yet Caitlin had seen the peace that stayed with the old woman until the end. Never had death seemed more friendly than at that moment when the woman quietly took her last breath and exhaled with a soft sigh, a tender smile on her lips.

Caitlin knew she was sad for herself, not the woman. She would miss their conversations, their sharing of healing with local herbs, and the old woman's wisdom that had been garnered over the years.

Never had her little clearing looked more peaceful to Caitlin, more inviting. Quietly she led Arturo to his stall and made sure that he was fed and had water before she quickly spread the feed for her chickens and went into the cabin.

The evening rays of the sun followed her through the door, lighting the shadows in the corners of the room and illuminating the figure who stood in front of the fireplace, waiting patiently for her.

"I told you I'd be back," Adam said quietly.

Seeing Adam again after the many weeks without him, together with the emotional strain she'd just undergone, were too much for Caitlin to handle at the moment. She burst into tears.

He was beside her in two long strides. Scooping her into his arms, he walked over to the bed and sat down, holding her close. "What's wrong, my love. Tell me."

His soft words only caused her tears to flow more freely, and she gave herself up to the luxury of Adam's arms and the joy of being comforted. She had not known when to expect him again. He could not have come at a time when she needed him more. Now that he was there, she no longer had to resist the ties they had forged during his stay with her.

"I didn't kid myself that you would be overjoyed to see me," he finally muttered, "but I didn't expect to reduce you to tears."

She slipped her arms around his neck and hugged him, holding him tightly as though afraid he would disappear. When the tears began to diminish, she leaned back slightly so that she could see him more clearly.

The weeks away had obviously done him good. He looked fit—tanned and healthy. She'd never seen him look better.

"Oh, Adam," she finally said. "I didn't know if you would really come."

"You should know me well enough to know I always do what I say." He glanced down at her arms, still locked around his shoulders. "I have the feeling," he said with a slight smile, "that you didn't forget me." With a hesitancy that she found endearing, he lowered his head and kissed her softly on her lips. "Does this mean that you're glad to see me?"

She smiled and nodded.

He rewarded her honesty with another kiss. He took his time letting her know how much he had missed her. Caitlin felt the muscles of his back bunch beneath her hands. She became aware of the strength in his shoulders and arms that held her so fiercely against him. Adam had come back. She recalled the number of nights she'd lain awake, remembering what it had been like to have him lying next to her in bed, and the many nights when her dreams had been full of him. How could she possibly resist him now that he was back with her?

Adam seemed to be trying to memorize her, his
hands ceaselessly roaming up and down her back,
from her shoulders to her hips, as though reassuring
himself that she really did exist and wasn't just a fig-
ment of his fevered imagination.

Her response to his kisses encouraged him to continue and he eased back on the bed until they were
lying there, side by side, their mouths still clinging,
enjoying the taste and touch of each other.

As though they had a mind of their own, his hands
slid from her back and lightly traced a line from the
hollow in her neck down between her breasts to her
waist, then paused. Her quickened breathing seemed
to match his own breathlessness.

He needed to get a rein on his emotions, now that
he was once again with her. He'd had several weeks to
plan what he would say and do once he saw her again,
but her tears and the obvious loss of control when she
saw him had unnerved him completely. He found
himself wanting to comfort her.

She seemed so relaxed with him, as though for the
first time she no longer fought her true feelings.

Caitlin began to pop open the snaps on his plaid
western shirt so that her hands could find the smooth
surface of his broad chest.

Her fingers touching his bare flesh caused him to
quiver. Surely she understood what that was doing to
him. If she did, she certainly didn't seem to care. She
was responding to his kisses as though she wanted
nothing more in life than to be there in his arms.

Which was fine with him.

When he found her breasts with his fingertips, he
felt her body jump in response, but rather than pull

back from him, she merely deepened the kiss. Adam could feel his heart racing. He needed to put a halt to what was happening. Now. Otherwise he would have no control over what happened next.

Her blouse lay open, exposing her breasts, and she leaned closer to him so that they touched his bare chest. He groaned, unable to fight the feelings that were rapidly overtaking him.

"Caitlin, love—"

She paused and looked into his eyes, seeing the love and burning desire, feeling the same emotions stirring deeply within her.

"I love you, Adam," she murmured, her lips pressing against his cheek and ear.

With those words, Adam forgot all about practicing restraint in favor of expressing his love for her in the most physical way possible.

He smoothed her blouse off her shoulders so that her upper body was revealed to him. Her skin glowed with a satiny sheen, her translucent coloring in deepest contrast to her fiery hair which lay in disordered confusion around her head and shoulders.

He traced the scar that followed the line of her shoulder, pleased to see that it had healed well. Then he leaned over and kissed it.

She was so beautiful, even more beautiful than he'd remembered, and he had forgotten nothing about her during their time apart.

He felt her heart fluttering in her chest when his mouth rested on the pink tip of her breast. He felt as though he held a frightened bird in his arms. His tongue lightly flicked over her breast, and he watched her body's response.

Caitlin feverishly explored his shoulders and chest with her fingertips, still in a daze at his presence. His heavy shoulder muscles felt so comforting somehow, and she sighed when his mouth encircled her breast.

Eventually Adam paused long enough to slide off his boots, then he quickly removed the rest of his clothing. He gazed down at her with a possessiveness that seemed to scorch her with its warmth, while at the same time left her feeling shy and uncertain. Without saying a word, he slipped off her pants and shoes, and she felt the cool evening air against her bared skin. She shivered, more from nerves than anything else.

Adam picked her up, pulled back the covers of the bed, and slipped her between them, crawling in beside her.

Had he said anything to her, anything at all, Caitlin might have been able to get a grip on her emotions, but it became obvious that Adam was a man of action, not words. And his actions made it clear how he still felt about her.

Not that he rushed her. On the contrary, he seemed to feel as though they had all the time in the world. If she tensed when he touched Caitlin in a new area, he would pause, then continue to stroke her until she relaxed.

Her body responded to his touch while he gave her slow, intoxicating kisses, reassuring her on the deepest, most fundamental level that he would never hurt her.

By the time he was poised above her, Caitlin watched him with fascinated eyes, her breathing ragged, her skin warm from his touch.

Adam slowly lowered himself to her and wasn't in the least surprised to discover that no one had been there before him. He'd been aware of her innocence on some subconscious level, had known of her purity. He touched her lightly, hoping not to frighten her.

Her eyes widened at the unexpected pressure and the sensation of him, so intimately pressed against her.

"It's all right, my love," he soothed. "Just relax. Everything's just fine."

When he took possession of her body, Caitlin discovered that he was right. Because of his loving concern and his inexhaustible patience, she was ready for him. Once the initial discomfort was past, Caitlin was swept away with the sense of release and freedom of expression.

She had never experienced anything resembling the feelings Adam aroused in her. He was so much an extension of her own being that for the first time in her life she realized what it meant to be one with another person.

He seemed to know what to do to increase the pleasurable feelings that were sweeping over her, and she clung to him as though to a lifeboat—clinging so she wouldn't be swept completely away into the sea of sensation rolling over them both.

Caitlin seemed to know instinctively how to respond to him. She met each of his movements with one of her own, delighting in the recognition of what her responsiveness did to him. He seemed to have such control and mastery over them both. Suddenly there was no more caution or patience. He caught fire, causing her to burst into flames, as well.

By the time Caitlin could comprehend what had happened, Adam was drawing slow, deep breaths, his head resting on the pillow next to hers, his body slumped to her side so that his weight was only partially on her. She felt bemused lying in his arms—as though she had spent most of her life there and that it was the most natural place in the world to be.

She studied his face as she'd seen him so often, with his eyes closed, and realized how differently he looked now. His long lashes still hid his expression, but his face was fuller, the scar almost invisible, and his color was very healthy. In fact, he looked flushed, which might be due to the exertion he'd recently undergone.

When his eyes finally opened, she was surprised to see the rueful, contrite expression in them.

"Will you forgive me, love? Because I'm not at all sure I can forgive myself."

She leaned closer and kissed him lightly. "There's nothing to forgive."

"You probably won't believe that I didn't have this all planned."

"I know."

"Are you okay?"

"I'm fine."

He stroked her back. "I came back to convince you that I love you. I wanted you to know that you can trust me." He shook his head ruefully. "I have a funny way of showing it."

"Why do you want me to trust you?"

"Because I have a favor to ask of you."

"Okay. Ask."

Adam eyed her thoughtfully and said, "It isn't going to be easy for you."

"All right," she responded calmly.

"You told me that you saw the man who drove the car the night I was almost killed."

"Yes."

"You said he was also the gunman who shot you."

"Yes."

He paused for a moment, uncertain. "I need you to identify him for me."

She smiled at his serious expression. "I'll do whatever I can to help."

Adam gained enough confidence in her calm acceptance to continue. "What I need you to do is to go to San Antonio with me, look through the tons of pictures we keep on file and see if we have him in our records." Anxiously he watched her face for some reaction.

Caitlin was quiet for several minutes, knowing that whatever decision she made would have an irrevocable impact on her life. Did she have the courage to do what needed to be done?

Adam took her hand and softly kissed the palm. "I know how you feel about leaving here. But I would be with you, love. I want you to come to Texas with me so much. These last few weeks have been hell without you."

I know only too well what it's been like without you, Caitlin silently answered. *I'm not sure I'm strong enough to allow you to leave me a second time.*

"I love you, Caitlin. I want to marry you and take you home to live with me."

Not marriage, Adam, she protested silently. *We can't take that risk.*

"Would you at least give our relationship a chance? I promise to bring you back the minute you want to come."

What could she say? She wanted to find the man who had tried to kill him. Until the man was apprehended, Adam wouldn't be safe. Caitlin couldn't live with the thought that he was still in danger without doing everything in her power to help him.

Then what choice did she have? Adam needed her. Caitlin had faced the truth of their strong ties weeks ago. Today had merely strengthened them, pointing out something important to her.

She needed Adam, too.

His eyes were filled with concern as he watched her. She felt the love and warmth that emanated from him. Caitlin reminded herself that she wouldn't be alone. Adam would be there if she became overwhelmed. After all this time on her own, perhaps she would be better able to cope with what she sensed and felt around her.

"When do you want to leave?" she finally asked.

Adam let out an Indian war cry, the kind that had echoed over the Texas plains a century ago. He rolled over in bed, holding her tightly against him, until he lay over her, staring down into her flushed face, his own face radiating his delight with her decision.

"We'll leave in the morning, darlin'. I have no intention of moving out of this bed until then."

Caitlin could find nothing to complain about in that statement.

Seven

———

The gently rolling hills of central Texas were already baking in the sun, although the calendar insisted summer wouldn't arrive for a few more weeks.

Now that they were nearing the ranch, Caitlin could feel herself growing nervous. The drive north had been uneventful. Adam explained that the car was new, and she realized something that she'd given no thought to before—money was no problem in Adam's life.

She refused to dwell on the fact that he wanted to marry her. One step at a time. She had agreed to the visit.

The frustrating part about her abilities was the way her emotions interfered with her reception of messages. Seldom could Caitlin visualize what was happening in her own life or how things would work out. It didn't seem fair, somehow, since she felt more afflicted than blessed with the awareness in the first place.

One thing she knew for certain: Adam had made a definite claim on her. There was no denying his intentions. Since his arrival at the cabin two days ago, he'd rarely let her get more than an arm's length away from him.

Adam had openly revealed the more sensuous side of his nature to Caitlin, surprising her when she remembered the control he had kept on himself during the weeks they had been together. Now that the control had been lifted, Caitlin found herself with a man who couldn't seem to get enough of her.

She understood the feeling. Caitlin had never desired a physical relationship before, never missed or regretted that she and Rick had never made love.

Now, thanks to Adam, she had discovered a means of expressing her emotions in a physical manner, and she reveled in the experience. Adam appeared delighted with her response to his lovemaking and her willingness to share herself with him.

She knew she'd hurt him by not agreeing to marry him. It wasn't from lack of love. If anything, her hesitancy was because she loved him too much to agree to something that might not make him happy. After all, he had seen her only in her own controlled environment. Her agreement to come to Texas with him was in the nature of an experiment.

If she could handle living around people again, then they had a foundation to build a marriage. Adam's passionate lovemaking had gone a long way to convincing her that they belonged together. Perhaps he had known that. She knew she couldn't find it in her heart to regret his possession of her. All she could hope was that their love for each other would be strong enough to ease them through the coming visit.

Her mind kept returning to the night he'd arrived. They hadn't gotten much sleep. Adam had kept reaching for her in the night, as though to make sure she was really there beside him.

"I don't know how I managed not to make love to you before I left," he had said to her the next morning. Caitlin lay limply on top of him, while he stroked her back soothingly. He'd just completed another rather comprehensive lesson in lovemaking.

"I wouldn't have stopped you," she admitted in a shy burst of honesty.

"But you wouldn't have left with me, either. I knew that. I couldn't handle loving you, then leaving."

"Then you must have been confident yesterday that I would agree to go back with you."

"No. If you had refused, I would have stayed here."

She raised her head from his shoulder and stared at him in surprise.

He smiled at the expression on her face. "You are a part of my life, Caitlin. You will always be a part of me. If you find that you can't live in my world, then I intend to live in yours. I will not give you up."

That conversation kept running through her head while Caitlin watched the Texas hill country roll by. For the first time she faced how cowardly her actions had been, by insisting on remaining in the mountains. Adam had put their relationship first. He was determined to work out everything else.

She admired that trait in him. There was so much about Adam that she admired. She looked over at him, and his eyes met hers for a brief glance before returning to the road.

"Tired?"

"A little."

"We should be there in another hour." He took his hand from the wheel and brushed his knuckles against her cheek. "You didn't get much sleep last night."

"Neither did you."

"I know. But I'm not complaining."

"What have you told your family about me, Adam?"

"That you're a very special person and that I love you very much." His warm tone seemed to ease the tension within her.

Her relaxed state lasted until they turned off the highway and followed a winding country road that Adam mentioned led to the ranch. She straightened slightly and studied the surrounding area carefully. This was home to Adam. He wanted her to share it with him.

When they pulled up into the ranch yard, Caitlin looked around in dismay at the size of the place.

The two-story house had been built in another era, when labor and material were cheap. A long porch wrapped around three sides of the house. There was also a large barn, a few pens, and several pieces of machinery sitting around. The ranch looked almost as large as the small village where she traded for supplies.

As soon as the car stopped, the screen door of the house flew open, and a young woman came out. Caitlin immediately recognized Felicia. Without a doubt the woman was beautiful with her long blond hair and green eyes. What Adam hadn't thought to mention and Caitlin hadn't known was that Felicia was pregnant.

Caitlin felt a sudden sense of identification with Felicia, and she wondered if it was due to the resemblance between the brother and sister. Adam opened the car door and helped Caitlin out. With his arm around her shoulders, he guided her to the house where Felicia waited.

"Caitlin, this is my sister, Felicia." He leaned over and kissed Felicia. "Here she is, sis. I managed to convince her to come for a visit."

Felicia's smile reminded Caitlin even more of Adam, and when Felicia held out her hand, Caitlin found her words echoing her thoughts. "You and Adam look so much alike."

Felicia laughed, a happy sound that warmed Caitlin's heart. Felicia hugged her brother tightly for a moment. "I consider that a compliment, but big brother here seems to think he's been insulted every time anyone mentions the family resemblance."

"I don't, either," Adam retorted. He glanced around and asked, "Is Dane around?"

"He should be back within the hour. Had to run into town for something. We didn't expect to see you this early." She motioned for them to go into the house ahead of her. "Would you like something to drink? How was the trip? Did you run into any bad weather? Dane said—"

"Whoa! Wait a minute!" Adam protested. "One thing at a time, will you? Yes, we'd love to have something to drink, the trip was fine, the weather was great, and what did Dane say?"

The two of them continued their banter as they moved along the wide hallway. Caitlin peered into open doors as they went by. She saw a long living room, dining room, a den and office, then found herself in the kitchen while Adam held out a chair for her.

Felicia poured each of them a large glass of iced tea. After placing a sprig of mint in each one and setting a saucer with sliced lemons on the table, she sat down at the table and smiled at the two of them.

"I'm so glad you came, Caitlin. Adam was worried you wouldn't."

Caitlin glanced at Adam. He was leaning back against his chair, looking relaxed and happy. She'd never really seen him that way before. She liked the look on him; he wore it very well.

"I'm glad I came, too," she agreed softly.

"I've put you in my old room. It's got a nice view of the place. If you aren't too tired later, I'd like to take you over to see the house Dane and I are building. It's about two miles down the road from here, overlooking the river." She glanced at Adam and shook her head. "It would probably never occur to Adam to reassure you that if you decide to settle here you aren't going to have to share your home with a bunch of relatives."

So Adam has told Felicia he wants to marry me, Caitlin realized. She felt the pressure of knowing that others were also waiting for her decision. Caitlin cast around for a way to change the subject, and she remembered the fact that Felicia was pregnant.

Her mind filled with images, and she knew that Dane and Felicia were delighted. They wanted a family. She smiled at the turbulent relationship the two had shared for years. Impulsively she leaned toward Felicia and patted her hand.

"I know Dane wants a boy, Felicia," she said with a mischievous grin, "but he's going to love his daughter very much. The boys will come later."

Adam and Felicia stared at her in stunned silence, and Caitlin suddenly realized what she'd said. Why had she spoken the thought out loud? She could see Dane with his tiny black-haired daughter, and the love and laughter they shared like a shimmering light around them. Caitlin had spoken without thinking about the consequences of her words.

Adam was the first one to break the charged silence. "Uhh, Felicia, I did forget to mention one thing about Caitlin. You see, she, uh—"

"You already know I'm going to have a girl?" Felicia said, interrupting Adam as though she hadn't heard him.

Caitlin could feel the tension begin to build behind her eyes. Oh, no. She hadn't been there five minutes, and already she'd managed to create a problem.

She forced herself to meet Felicia's startled gaze. "I seem to have the ability of knowing things like that," she explained with a sigh.

Felicia clapped her hands in delight. "But that's wonderful." She turned to Adam. "Why didn't you tell us sooner, Adam? What an amazing gift. Have you always had it?"

Caitlin gazed at Felicia in surprise. She didn't seem to be shocked or upset. Nor did she seem to question the validity of the statement. She was sincerely interested, and was waiting for Caitlin to respond.

Caitlin soon found that for every question she answered, Felicia had three more for her. It didn't matter. Caitlin felt accepted as she was slowly drawn into the loving circle shared by Adam and Felicia.

Having already talked about her background with Adam, Caitlin discovered it was much easier to discuss it now. Neither one of them treated her as some freak. She began to relax and enjoy herself, even drawing laughs with some of her stories about her early days in the mountains.

When Dane walked into the room, he found his wife and brother-in-law chatting with a glowing young woman with bright red-gold hair cascading over her shoulders, her face animated and her eyes sparkling. He had no trouble understanding why Adam had fallen head over heels in love. The man had taste, he'd give him that.

Caitlin glanced up and saw the tall, good-looking man leaning against the doorjamb. She smiled. He straightened up and said, "It looks like the St. Clairs are at it again, both talking nonstop." Sauntering over to Felicia, he kissed her, then held out his hand to Adam. "Good to see you managed to get down to Mexico and back this time without any trouble."

Felicia was the first one to respond. "Oh, Dane, I want you to meet Caitlin Moran. Caitlin, this is my lord and master, Dane Rineholt."

Dane pulled a chair out from the table and sat down, leaning back in obvious contentment. "You can't appreciate the irony in that statement yet, Caitlin, but when you get to know her better, you will. Nobody even tries to dominate Felicia." He glanced at Adam. "No one would dare try, right?"

The men grinned at each other, and Caitlin felt the love that was shared between these three people and had a sudden yearning to be a part of their magic circle. Was it possible?

Adam glanced at his watch. "I hadn't realized how long we've been sitting here talking. I haven't even taken Caitlin upstairs to unpack or rest." He stood up and held out his hand to her. "Let me give you a quick tour of the place, love." He glanced over at the couple still seated. "We'll see you later."

Adam kept her close to his side while he showed Caitlin the main floor of the house, explaining the various additions that had been made to the original structure. Then he took her upstairs and down the hall to her bedroom.

The room was beautifully old-fashioned, with a colorful quilt decorating the four-poster and a braided rug on the floor. Caitlin scarcely had time to see it before Adam pulled her into his arms and began kissing her—deep, soul-searching kisses that caused Caitlin to forget everything but the man who seemed to be a part of her, body and soul. When he finally lifted his mouth from hers, they were both short of breath. "I've been wanting to do that for the past several hours. You've become an addiction to me. The more I have of you, the more I want."

Caitlin felt the same way but didn't want to admit how weak she was. One of them needed to hang on to some perspective. However, she did feel more at ease now that she had actually come into Adam's home and met his family.

The meeting hadn't been as bad as she'd expected. They accepted her and seemed sincerely pleased that she and Adam had found each other. Caitlin began to believe there was a chance that she and Adam could work out their lives so they could be together.

"I know you're tired," he said, rubbing her back with a gentle hand. "Why don't you stretch out for a while and try to get some rest. We'll spend the weekend here and drive into San Antonio on Monday. My boss, Rob McFarlane, is most interested in meeting you."

"Does he know about my psychic abilities?"

"No. I haven't told him because I didn't want you to feel uncomfortable. If you want to tell him, fine. Otherwise, he thinks you saw the driver well enough to identify him. We'll have you go through the pictures and see if you recognize him." He walked over to the window and looked out. "Don't take on more than you are comfortable with, love. Just know I'm here, that I'll always be here, and that I love you."

He turned around and headed for the door.

"I'm not going to kiss you again. If I do, I'll end up on that bed with you, and that's no way to set an example for my sister!" he said with a grin.

Caitlin slipped off her shoes and dress and lay down, pulling a light blanket across her. She had a hunch that Felicia would not be at all shocked to know she and Adam had slept together. But she supposed there was no reason to shatter a brother's illusions about his sister's innocence.

"Dane?" Felicia got up from her chair as soon as Adam and Caitlin left the kitchen and walked around the table to her tall, dark-haired husband. Sinking down into his lap, she curled her arms around his neck. "I've got some news for you that I'm not at all sure you're going to like."

"What's that?"

"You aren't getting a son the first time around."

He looked at her with a puzzled expression on his face. "What are you talking about?"

"I'm going to have a girl."

He laughed. "Who says?"

"Caitlin."

"Caitlin? And how would she know?"

"She just knows. That's what she and Adam have been trying to explain to me since they arrived. Caitlin is different, Dane. She sees things, she knows things, that most other people don't know. She saw you with a black-haired daughter, and she also sees us with sons. I'm afraid she predicts a rather large family."

He grinned. "Is that supposed to scare me or something? Remember, I come from a large family myself."

"I know. It doesn't scare me, either. But having someone around who knows those kinds of things is going to take some getting used to."

"Why? There are many people who have a sense of things to happen. Perhaps Caitlin has a stronger sense of it. Doesn't every family have someone who could always tell when it was going to storm, or knew about a death before it happened, or identified who was calling on the phone before they answered it?"

"Well, maybe, but not like this."

"Maybe not exactly, but it doesn't make her strange or that different. What it makes her is sensitive to other people."

"Have you ever known anyone like Caitlin?"

"When I was in the service, I was stationed with a fella from Arizona, an Indian, who had an uncanny ability of predicting what was going to happen. Managed to save my life a couple of times with his predictions. I got cut off from the rest of my unit once and would have been left if he hadn't known where to look for me."

"You never told me about that."

"No. But I definitely believe in man's extra senses. I think we've always had them, but as we've grown more civilized, we've used them less and less until they've grown dormant. I think it's possible for anyone to increase their extrasensory skills with practice and a certain amount of skill in learning to focus their attention."

"I can't get over the change in Adam since he met Caitlin."

"In what way?"

"I'm not sure. He's more relaxed somehow, as though he knows what he wants and how he intends to get it. It's as though he's always known that sooner or later he would find her. Adam has always been popular with women, but he never got serious with anybody. And yet as soon as he met Caitlin, he fell like a boulder, immediately and with little warning."

"I was the same way."

"Who are you kidding? You played around for years!"

"No. I *waited* around for years. I knew as soon as I first laid eyes on you that I was going to marry you. I just had to wait forever for you to grow up."

She leaned over and kissed him, a very loving, lingering kiss. When she finally pulled away from him, she noticed that he hadn't opened his eyes. "It was worth the wait, though, wasn't it?" she teased.

"You're damned right," he agreed, blindly searching for her mouth once more.

Dinner was a hilarious affair. The four of them found all sorts of subjects to discuss. By unspoken agreement, no one brought up the planned trip to San Antonio or its purpose. Instead Dane and Felicia enjoyed telling Caitlin all about Adam as a boy and later, as a young man. Adam retaliated by describing the relentless war waged between Dane and Felicia before they acknowledged the love that had been between them for years.

By the time Caitlin prepared for bed that night, she knew that she could be very happy living in this house with Adam, with Felicia and Dane nearby.

Her years on the mountain had given her time to come to terms with her heightened awareness, and she no longer felt intimidated by the knowledge that seemed to flow through her at unexpected times.

Now she was going to put that knowledge to use by trying to find who had tried to kill Adam. And why. The why was even more important. Somehow she knew the motive was the key to the whole business.

By the time she fell asleep, Caitlin knew that the following few days would be a turning point in her life. She only hoped she was ready for it.

Eight

Adam's mood was cheerful and teasing during the trip to San Antonio. Caitlin found his lightheartedness contagious. She couldn't remember the last time she'd been so relaxed and happy. Her weekend at the ranch had brought back memories of how she'd felt as a young girl—full of fun and high spirits.

Adam's sudden appearance in her life had been like a bomb bursting—shattering her routine and her views of herself and the world around her. He'd given her the courage to venture out of the safe nest she had created.

"I hope the weekend wasn't too much for you," Adam said, effectively ending the silence. "You haven't said anything since we left home."

"Oh, no. I enjoyed it very much. Dane and Felicia are very special people."

"They enjoyed you, as well."

"I was just thinking..."

"About what?"

"That it might be nice to be married at the ranch."

The car made a sudden swerve before it continued down the highway.

"You pick a hell of a time to accept a marriage proposal, lady. At the moment, I can't do a damn thing about it."

Caitlin looked over at him, her face glowing. "What do you want to do about it?"

Adam gave her a brief glance, then returned his attention to the highway. "I'd much prefer to show you than to tell you." That brief glance raised her temperature considerably.

Admitting that she wanted to marry him seemed to lift a weight off her shoulders. Somehow she had to believe that what they felt for each other was strong enough to weather whatever life presented to them.

They spent the remaining miles discussing dates, making plans for the ceremony and what to do with Caitlin's animals. One of the teenagers in the village had agreed to feed and look after Arturo, Chula, the goat and the chickens while she was gone. Now they would need to make permanent arrangements.

Adam insisted they go shopping and buy her a ring before going to the office. Once in town, they stopped, and he called Rob from a pay phone. Hanging up after a brief conversation, he laughed and caught her in his arms.

"Rob said a few hours wasn't going to make that much difference and if I'd managed to talk you into an engagement, I might as well get the evidence on your finger."

He took her hand and began to lead her through the large shopping mall. "Let's have lunch first, then we'll get started. I know just what I want for you."

By the time they reached the Agency office, Caitlin felt her thoughts almost whirling. The unaccustomed crowds, as well as Adam's excitement, seemed to put an electrical charge around her. She was relieved to discover that with conscious effort she could block out the snippets of impressions that came through, in the same manner that she ignored bits and pieces of conversation reaching her ear while they moved through the different stores.

Glancing down at the large diamond solitaire, Caitlin could scarcely believe how quickly Adam had gotten organized once she agreed to his proposal. The man striding down the hall beside her was a definite force to be reckoned with.

She found the Agency office a peaceful contrast to the busy mall. The sound of a typewriter in another office—muffled and indistinct—was the only noise that penetrated the quietness of the rooms.

When Adam ushered Caitlin into Robert McFarlane's office and closed the door, even the noise of the typewriter faded away, and Caitlin's frayed nerves felt soothed by the silence.

After the introductions Rob motioned for them to be seated. "I'm very pleased that you agreed to come to San Antonio and help us out, Miss Moran. From what Adam told me on the phone, he's managed to talk you into more than a visit to the Lone Star State."

Caitlin saw Adam shift slightly in his chair and realized with amusement that Adam was embarrassed. She smiled at Rob. "I would like to help in whatever way I can."

"Has Adam explained to you what was happening at the time of his disappearance?"

"No. I never asked."

"He had managed to become friends with Felipe Santiago under the guise of helping to distribute drugs on this side of the river. Santiago was the middleman between the South American contacts and the distribution to the north. After a few successful operations, Santiago had learned to trust Adam."

She looked at the men in dismay. "You mean you were actually bringing the drugs in and distributing them?"

"We brought them in and impounded them. Of course, Santiago wasn't aware of that. Adam had told Santiago he wanted to meet his contact from South America, and Santiago arranged a meeting. That meeting was aborted, although Santiago never knew that, because of a message Adam received just before he left his hotel."

Rob paused for a moment and then continued, "Adam got a call telling him the meeting was a trap, that Santiago was afraid Adam was getting greedy and trying to bypass him. The caller said he could give him the evidence he needed without risk if Adam would agree to meet him somewhere away from Monterrey."

"So that's why Adam was in the mountains?" she offered.

"Yes."

"Only he never kept his appointment."

"No. What we want to know is who knew about the appointment in the mountains. Was is another plot of Santiago's, or is someone else involved? The bottom line here is—does someone know that Adam is an agent, or were they just trying to get rid of competition in the drug trade? I can't send him back over there until I know for certain. That's where you come in."

"If I can identify the man for you, you'll know why he was trying to kill Adam?"

"That's what we're counting on, yes."

"And if I can't identify him?"

"We're in no worse shape than we were before. The thing is, we've run out of leads."

"I see. I appreciate your explaining all of this to me, Mr. McFarlane."

"If you were merely a witness, I wouldn't have, believe me. But as Adam's future wife I wanted you to understand the importance of the situation. He didn't have the clearance to give you the details. I do." He stood up and held out his hand.

"It's been a pleasure to meet you, and I won't hold you up any further. The job ahead of you is long and tedious."

Caitlin followed Adam down a long hallway to another office. Two desks were pushed together in the center of a small room.

"Zeke Taylor and I share this office whenever we're in town, which isn't very often," Adam explained. "Have a seat, and I'll bring in the albums for you to go over. Do you want anything to drink?"

"Not at the moment," she replied, sitting down and looking around. "Where's Zeke now?"

"Mexico, as far as I know. He rarely comes out anymore. He's been with the Agency for years and has developed a damned good cover down there. He doesn't want to do anything to jeopardize it."

He leaned over and kissed her. "I'll be back shortly."

Caitlin closed her eyes and tried to blank out her thoughts, but it was difficult. She saw Adam everywhere: his high spirits in the mall; the beauty of his male body the night he made such exquisite love to her; lying unconscious for those endless days and nights; the look of horror on his face just before his car was hit.

Adam seemed to fill her whole mind. She had never felt anything so powerful before. Yet she knew she had to clear away all of those emotions so that her mind would be free to pick up what she could.

Hours later Caitlin finally had to call a halt to the progression of photographs Adam kept handing her. "I'm sorry, Adam. I can't look at them any longer. This is getting to be more than I can handle at the moment."

Adam took one look at her face and realized he'd been pushing her. She was very pale, and her eyes had a bruised quality about them. "Damn. I wasn't thinking. I'm afraid I get carried away once I start on something like this. You must be exhausted."

"I am, but not because of the number of pictures you've shown me. These people carry such a charge on them I can almost feel their presence when I look at their photograph." She pointed to one. "He's in prison now and filled with hate." She indicated another one. "He's extremely dangerous. Kills for the excitement of it." About a third one, she said, "I don't think he's around any longer. There's a strong possibility he's dead."

Adam stared at her in surprise. "I guess I hadn't given it a thought—how all of this would affect you." He ran his hand through his hair, not for the first time that afternoon, and sighed. "I can't seem to understand what you do and how you do it, yet I love you completely. I can better see why you're touchy about your abilities. They definitely give a sense of supernatural."

He stood up and held out his hand to her. "Come on. I'll buy you dinner and ply you with wine. That's bound to help you relax. Then I'll take you to a hotel and let you get some rest."

He was as good as his word. By the time they walked into the hotel room, Caitlin felt much more relaxed and more than a little sleepy. The good food and wine had certainly done the trick.

She kicked off her shoes and began to unbutton her blouse while Adam adjusted the thermostat and drapes. When he turned around, he discovered she wore only her panties and a bra. He watched her as she walked into the bathroom and turned on the shower.

He cleared his throat slightly. "I'll stop by in the morning so we can have breakfast together."

Caitlin glanced around in surprise. "You aren't staying with me tonight?"

"I know you're tired and—"

"That doesn't matter. It would be nice to know you're nearby."

He wondered if she had any idea how enticing she looked standing there. "You don't understand, Caitlin. I used up all the willpower I had during the weeks I spent at the cabin with you. I love you too much to be able to spend the night with you without making love to you, especially now.''

With deliberate movements she calmly unfastened her bra and stepped out of her panties. "No one asked you to exercise any willpower, Adam.'' With a lingering glance over her shoulder, she stepped into the spray of the shower.

Adam needed no further encouragement.

Caitlin looked around in surprise a few minutes later when she heard the shower door slide open. Adam stepped in, wearing only a grin.

''Are you enjoying the convenience of a shower after all those years without one?'' he asked with studied nonchalance as he took the soapy washcloth away from her. He began to lightly stroke her arms, her shoulders and, with ever widening circles, her breasts.

Caitlin felt a shiver race through her at his touch. He had such a strong effect on her. When his hands slipped across her stomach and rested at the top of her thighs, she couldn't repress the slight moan of pleasure at his touch.

''Something wrong?''

''Uh-uh,'' she murmured, unable to find any words.

''Am I disturbing you in some way?''

She looked up at him. "What do you think?''

His hands went around her, pulling her closer until her soap-slickened body pressed against him. He meticulously soaped her back from shoulder to hip, but his touch felt more like a caress than an impersonal bathing.

When Adam finally leaned down and kissed her, her knees gave way, and she would have fallen if he hadn't held her even tighter against him. She twined her arms around his neck and returned his kiss with whole-hearted enthusiasm.

Adam felt the difference in her from their first time together. Her uninhibited response made it clear she felt committed to him and their future. He hadn't thought it possible to love her more than he did, but now his heart threatened to explode with the joy that flooded over him.

She insisted on taking her turn at bathing him and took such an excruciatingly long and loving time to soap his body that he thought he'd lose his mind with all the sensations sweeping through him.

When he'd had all he could take, Adam stepped away from her, turned her toward the water so she could rinse off, then gently pushed her out of the shower. After quickly rinsing off, he immediately followed.

After a couple of careless wipes with a towel, Adam picked her up and strode into the other room. "I've had all the teasing I intend to take from you, young lady," he said in a fierce voice. He dropped her on the bed.

"Who says I was teasing, Mr. St. Clair?"

His breath caught in his throat when he took in the picture she made. The dark blue of the spread was a stark contrast to her bright hair and shining eyes. Her pale skin still glistened from the shower, and with a feeling bordering on reverence, he knelt beside her and began to kiss her—starting with her neck, then her breasts, and slowly downward, pausing to nip her with his teeth and stroke her with his tongue.

His touch set off sparks all around her, and she felt as though her body had caught on fire. "Oh, Adam—"

"Do you love me?" he asked between kisses.

"Oh, yes."

"Do you want me?" He continued to drive her crazy with his mouth.

"Desperately."

"Then show me, sweet Caitlin. Show me what you want—show me how to please you."

With breathless sighs and soft words she let him know what his touch did to her and how much she needed him.

There was nothing gentle about their lovemaking this time. It was an expression of powerful love mingled with need. Neither one of them could get enough of the other during the ensuing hours. Their murmured whispers spoke of their joy with each other, their hope for the future, their unquenchable love.

All of Caitlin's fears and concerns were exorcised during the night. She'd been given a second chance to embrace life. This time she intended to take it.

Something woke her from a sound sleep, and Caitlin sat up in bed, alarmed. She looked around, dazed, trying to figure out where she was. Then she remembered. She was in San Antonio with Adam.

Glancing down at her side, Caitlin smiled. Adam lay on his stomach, his head almost buried under his pillow. The covers lay low on his back, barely covering his hips. He looked so comfortable.

Frowning, she tried to decide what had awakened her. She felt a niggling feeling in the back of her mind—a warning about something.

Getting out of bed carefully, so as not to awaken Adam, she slipped on her robe, then went into the bathroom for a glass of water. When she walked back into the bedroom, she went over to the window and opened the curtains.

The skyline of San Antonio was in front of her. The sky was black and seemed to be filled with stars, and the words to a song she'd sung as a child came back to her—something about the stars at night being big and bright, deep in the heart of Texas.

She stood there and gazed out at the night, feeling a definite unease. Eventually she sat down in the large overstuffed chair by the window and leaned her head back.

Her mind had cleared, her emotions had been nourished and reciprocated by Adam's lovemaking, and she was finally at peace with herself and her world. While she sat there, pictures began to form. She saw the man whose picture she had tried to find today and as thoughts and ideas formed and re-formed, she understood why she hadn't seen him, why he wouldn't be there.

Other people came in and out. Scenes were enacted, and slowly she began to piece the sequence of events together. It was a story of deceit and betrayal, of greed and malice. Pain began to build up within her. Pain for Adam . . . and for herself.

Now she knew. And in order to protect Adam, she must tell him. Would he accept the truth? Was there any way she could prove to him that it *was* the truth?

He dealt with facts and evidence. She had no facts or evidence. Yet she had no choice. Adam had to know, and she would have to tell him.

Caitlin stared up into the night, trying to blank out her mind once more. She watched as the stars began to fade, as light began to filter across the sky, slowly forcing the night to retreat, accepting another day.

"Caitlin?" Adam had stirred in his sleep and reached for her. When he didn't find her, his eyes flew open, and he saw her sitting across the room. "What's wrong?"

"Nothing, I just couldn't sleep."

"Well, come back to bed, and I'll try to help you relax."

She chuckled at the hopeful tone in his voice. Caitlin got up and came over to the bed. Slipping off her robe, she crawled in beside him.

"I missed you," he said, wrapping his arms around her and pulling her close.

"I'm glad." She kissed him along his jawline until she reached the side of his mouth. Then her mouth lingered on his, her tongue teasing him until he took over the kiss. He took his time, tasting and loving her, teasing and nibbling at her lower lip.

Caitlin closed her mind to everything but Adam. She loved Adam and he loved her. They had this time together, these perfect, precious moments when the world couldn't intrude on them.

She would tell him. But not now. Let the morning sunlight usher in the new day. In the quiet of the early dawn, there would only be love and fulfillment and appreciation of each other.

Nine

Caitlin woke to the smell of coffee, and for a moment she thought she was back in the cabin. Then she remembered.

Rolling over, she opened her eyes and found Adam holding a cup of coffee and sitting on the bed.

"I was wondering if you intended to sleep all morning. I didn't mean to wear you out last night." His grin was full of mischief. Adam St. Clair was so full of life. He was enthusiastic about everything and loyal to those he gave his love and friendship to. It was that loyalty she had to disturb this morning.

Trying to gain some time, she accepted the cup of coffee he offered her and asked, "What time is it?"

"After ten."

She hadn't meant to sleep so long.

"Breakfast is here. I went ahead and ordered."

"Oh." She glanced over at the table, all set up. Hastily finishing the coffee, she slid out of bed, placing the cup on the bedside table.

"I'll be ready in a few minutes." She went into the bathroom and washed her face, brushed her hair and teeth and reminded herself that she could not be a coward. She would tell him . . . right after breakfast.

Caitlin dressed and sat down across from Adam whose face shone as though a thousand candles had been lit from within. Conversation was limited while both of them ate. Caitlin didn't realize how expressive her face was until Adam finally set his cup down and looked at her for a long moment. The candles slowly seemed to flicker out, and his face filled with strain.

"Are you going to tell me what's wrong?"

"What do you mean?"

"Something's bothering you. You couldn't sleep last night. You're quiet this morning. Are you sorry about last night? Or is it the engagement? Damn it, don't leave me out of your thoughts. Share them with me."

"I know who is trying to kill you."

Her quiet voice seemed to make the words more intense, and for a moment Adam just stared at her, wondering at her tone and the look of strain on her face.

"You're in considerable danger," she added.

He tried to lighten up the situation a little by joking. "If I didn't get the message the first time, the gunman certainly convinced me of that. So who is he?"

"The gunman isn't important. He's a hired killer. You don't have him in your records because he's never been booked. His territory is Mexico and points south. He's never been to the States."

"Do you know who hired him?"

This was the hard part, and she wasn't sure how to explain. "A friend of yours."

He laughed, a short sound that held no sign of amusement. "Right. A friend."

"I mean it, Adam. He's a man very close to you, and he's betrayed you, not once, but many times."

His stomach clenched as he stared at her. She was obviously upset. He knew she believed what she was saying. "Who?"

She was quiet for a few minutes, her eyes closed. When she began to speak, it was in a clear, detached voice—almost without emotion. "He's tall, but not quite as tall as you. He is American but has dark hair and eyes and can pass as a Latin. He wears a closely trimmed beard...quite a ladies' man." She opened her eyes and looked at him. "You know him very well. You've been with him often. You work together."

Adam stared at her in disbelief. That description fit only one man that he worked with, the one man that it couldn't possibly be. He was stunned. He had counted so much on Caitlin's help. He'd believed in her, trusted her abilities, and now she was coming up with something so totally absurd that he had no choice but to discount everything.

Fighting to keep his voice neutral, he said, "Do you by any chance know his name?"

She was quiet for a moment, shook her head slightly and said, "I'm not sure. I think it starts with a *T*. Maybe Tanner... or Tyler."

Damn, she was good. He'd give her that. He wondered how she managed to get the description so accurately, even down to the name.

"Zeke Taylor?"

"Taylor. Yes. That fits." She looked at him, waiting for his reaction, but he didn't have one. He sat there looking at her with a slight smile on his face without saying a word. He leaned forward and poured himself another cup of coffee, silently holding up the pot to her. She shook her head, and he set it down.

He wasn't taking this as she had expected. She thought he would be more upset. From everything she had seen the two men were very close.

"Zeke Taylor, huh?"

"Yes."

"Well, love, I'm afraid your psychic powers led you astray on this one, but that's all right. Nobody expects you to be a hundred-percent accurate."

"You don't believe me."

"Oh, I don't think you're lying. I'm sure you honestly believe what you're saying is the truth. You're just wrong, that's all."

"Am I?"

She sounded so aloof, not like the warm woman he'd held so close to him the night before. She even looked aloof, her face carefully expressionless. He hadn't meant to hurt her feelings. He knew how sensitive she was to her abilities, and he could understand that. He didn't want her to take personally his refusal to accept what she said.

Adam stood up and walked across the room, then turned around and faced her. He rubbed his neck wearily, trying to find the right words.

"There's no way you could know this, but Zeke and I have been working on this case for as long as I've been with the Agency. He's put in as many hours on this as I have. My God! He trained me, as far as that goes. I never made a move down there that he didn't know about."

"Yes, that fits. He needed to know what you were uncovering."

Her cool, unemotional voice infuriated him. Instead of accepting his explanation, she used it to strengthen her own position. He tried to stay calm, reminding himself that she was stubborn. It wouldn't help him if he lost his temper.

All right, he decided. He'd play along with her until he could point out the fallacy of what she was saying. "Caitlin, why would Zeke Taylor want me killed?"

"Because you found out too much about what was going on down there, more than he thought you would. You got too close to him."

"That doesn't make sense."

"You remember the man you were to meet the night you were almost killed? Taylor killed him."

"That's a lie!" He strode over to her. "The facts are that Zeke Taylor met the man after I disappeared and got the information that led to Santiago's arrest. Zeke Taylor was the one who solved the case!"

Caitlin stood and walked over to the window. What was happening was as bad as she had feared. She could agree with Adam that she'd made up what she'd said, and perhaps they could eventually ignore what had just happened. But this was one situation she couldn't run from.

Lifting her chin slightly, Caitlin turned and faced Adam, her gaze meeting his squarely. "No. Taylor already knew the information he gave about Santiago, Adam. He sacrificed Santiago. Taylor had to decide who was expendable, and he certainly wasn't going to turn himself in." She walked back to the table and absently toyed with one of the spoons lying there. "The man died because he intended to tell you about Taylor's involvement in the operation." Restless, she walked to the door, then turned and faced him once more. "Taylor has kept the smugglers informed of the Agency's movements for years. Periodically he throws someone to the Agency to keep them happy."

Adam stood there watching her as she wandered back to the window. She explained as she paced. "Santiago was never that heavily involved with the operation, you see. He was a bored businessman who enjoyed the excitement. Zeke used him to front his own involvement. Zeke's the one who vouched for you so that Santiago accepted you so readily into the operations. Zeke needed you where he could keep an eye on you."

A noise outside the window distracted Caitlin. She glanced down at the river running along beside the hotel and saw a mariachi band playing in one of the pleasure boats cruising by. The lighthearted music seemed to bring into sharp focus the heavy tension that filled the room.

Adam ignored the music drifting up from the river. Instead of allowing the noise to distract him, he forced himself to concentrate on Caitlin's words. He wouldn't allow his reaction to her words to surface.

Caitlin stepped away from the window and looked at Adam. "Zeke doesn't know how the man you were supposed to meet found out about him," she explained, "but when you called him that night and told him about the anonymous phone call, he knew he had to do something fast." Adam's face remained without expression, and she continued, "He got to the man first and tried to find out how he got the information, but lost his temper and killed the man before he found out."

Once again, she looked out the window, wishing she was down there with the relaxed and happy crowd, enjoying the music, anywhere but there in that room, throwing words like missiles at Adam. Yet she knew she had no choice but to tell it all.

Turning to the silent man who was watching her every move with quiet intensity, Caitlin said, "That's when Zeke realized he was going to have to eliminate you before you dug any deeper and found another source that would lead you to him." She walked over to him. "He underestimated you, Adam. You are much smarter and have a great deal more cunning than he gave you credit for." Studying the man she loved, Caitlin could feel the waiting stillness that seemed to be wrapped around him. She wanted so much for him to understand.

"Zeke Taylor has a flourishing business in Mexico, one that he doesn't intend to jeopardize over a little thing like friendship." Wishing there was a way to soften what had to be said, she continued, "He likes you, Adam, but you've become too much of a threat to him. As long as you're alive, he won't feel safe." In a musing tone she added, "He still can't figure out how you survived. He saw a picture taken of you at the scene of the crash and thought you were dead." Remembering how Adam looked when she'd found him, she could well understand Zeke's conclusion. "Later, when he discovered your body was gone, he decided not to take any chances and sent his gunman up in the mountains to look for you."

Adam felt almost numb with shock. His world seemed to have broken into small, unrecognizable pieces. His belief in his own perceptions and judgment had just received a shattering blow. He broke out in a cold sweat.

Zeke Taylor? Impossible. Zeke had taught him everything he knew. Took him under his wing when he first started. He and Zeke had become good friends. Zeke wanted him dead?

"I'm sorry, Adam."

He heard Caitlin's voice as though from somewhere far away. He forced himself to focus on her face. Her lovely, adorable, lying face.

She had to be lying. Not intentionally, of course, but the pain wasn't any less. Didn't she know what her farfetched ideas could do to a man? They could reduce him to a babbling idiot. Didn't she understand she couldn't go around making wild accusations against people, without a shred of proof? Where was her evidence? Some vision or other she'd picked up in her head? Caitlin expected him to calmly walk into Rob's office and explain that he knew Zeke was trying to kill him because Caitlin had seen it all in a dream?

Adam could feel the pain and frustration pulling at him. "Why didn't you tell me this at the very beginning, when I regained consciousness? If you're so damned psychic, why did you wait until now? You sat there in the office yesterday afternoon—in Zeke's chair, by the way—looking at all those pictures and not coming up with anything. So what are you trying to do now? Trying to make up for wasting our time? Well, this isn't the way to do it, Caitlin. You don't have to make up something, you don't have to tell a bunch of lies and destroy a friendship out of some misguided need to play God."

He felt as though he'd run for miles. His chest hurt, and he was having trouble breathing. He wanted to smash his fist into something. Dammit! She didn't understand! She was playing around with something that was too vital to be taken lightly.

Psychic responses should be treated as games and nothing more. Something to amuse your friends and family with. He wanted to calm down and try to talk to her, but he was too upset at the moment, not necessarily at her, but at the situation.

Caitlin stood up. "I never lied to you, Adam. I'm not lying to you now. I didn't pick up on Zeke Taylor before because I wasn't trying to solve anything. I had no desire to find out who was trying to kill you or why. I was just trying to keep you from dying."

She walked over to the window and stood there looking out. With her back to him, she said, "You understand now, don't you? Why I can't live around people? Why I can't have close friends or close ties of any kind? When I'm in the mountains, I can control the flow because there are so few people around."

When he didn't respond, she continued, her voice husky. "I know what you're feeling right now, you see. You're feeling betrayed and angry and hurt. And you resent the fact that I understand all of that, as though you have no privacy at all, no place to retreat until you can come to terms with what you're feeling.

"This is why I was so uncertain about marrying you. No one should have to live with someone like me. If it helps any, this is what I was trying to protect you from. I don't feel in the least godlike, I'm afraid. I've never felt more human in my life. You see, I loved you so much I ignored everything I'd so painfully learned over the years and tried to convince myself we could make a relationship work."

Adam felt overwhelmed with emotions. All he knew was that he needed to get away. Moving toward the door, he said, "Look, we're both upset right now. I need some time to think. I'm sure you do, too. Why don't you do some sight-seeing, and I'll be back later this afternoon? We can talk then."

She turned around and saw him standing there, his hand on the door, and knew she was seeing him for the last time. "I'll be fine, Adam. Go ahead and do what you need to do."

He nodded and walked out the door, closing it quietly behind him.

Caitlin sank down into the chair and stared out the window. The sky was a pale blue now, filled with bright sunlight. A couple of wispy clouds dotted the blue expanse.

She tried not to think about the pain that seemed to be growing inside of her, minute by minute. She needed to be able to think clearly before the pain took over and she could only feel.

Decisions needed to be made. The truth was, she realized, decisions had already been made. Now they needed to be acted upon. She got up and packed the few things she had taken out of her suitcase the night before.

Glancing down at the ring Adam had given her the day before, she carefully slipped it off her finger. She couldn't leave it lying loose in the room. There was no sense in tempting one of the maids.

She placed it in an envelope furnished by the hotel, sealed it and put the envelope in Adam's bag. He'd see it when he packed.

Making sure she hadn't left anything that was hers, Caitlin left the room. She tried to think of what she had to do before she could allow herself to feel anything. Go to the airport. Get a plane to Monterrey. Hire a car to take her as far as the village, hike back to her cabin.

Rebuild her old life.

While she waited for the plane at the airport, one thought filtered through the careful blankness of her mind.

I must have needed to experience the loss of our love as strongly as Adam needed to experience the betrayal of a friend. She wondered why life's lessons seemed to come so hard.

Adam walked for several hours without any idea where he was. When he stopped, he realized that he had been following the scenic River Walk, ignoring the other people, his mind wrestling with the shock he'd received that morning.

He knew he'd overreacted. He'd known that at the time. Caitlin hadn't been to blame, and yet he'd accused her of lying, of all kinds of nonsensical things. Even though he didn't understand Caitlin's perceptions, he did know that she was sincere and had only been trying to help.

That was the key, he was sure. Because she wanted to help so much, she had forced some sort of "pick up" that she had misread...misinterpreted... something.

He glanced at his watch and realized it was almost three o'clock. Rob expected them in before now, but he knew Caitlin wouldn't be in the mood to look at any more pictures. Neither was he.

But he needed to go in. Wishing that Dane were there to discuss this with, he headed to the office. When he arrived, Rob's secretary smiled and said, "You're supposed to go on in whenever you show up, I believe were his words."

Adam knew he was going to hear about not coming in until midafternoon the day after he got himself engaged. Schooling his expression not to reveal his thoughts, he tapped at the door and opened it at the same time.

The man seated across from Rob wore a Mexican shirt, faded jeans and Mexican sandals. His wide smile flashed white in contrast to his close-trimmed beard when he saw Adam standing in the doorway. He dropped his feet off the desk where he'd had them propped and stood up. Throwing his arms around Adam, he hugged him and said, "Well, *mi amigo*,

Rob tells me congratulations are in order. I can't believe it, you old reprobate. You're finally going to settle down.''

"Hello, Zeke, what brings you back to the States?" He asked in a neutral tone.

Adam noticed that Rob and Zeke looked at each other in surprise, then back at him.

"Don't tell me you've already had your first quarrel," Rob asked half seriously.

"Something like that," Adam admitted, pulling up a chair and sitting down. "So what's up?"

When Rob realized Adam wasn't going to explain the mood he was in, he shrugged and said, "Oh, I was just trying to fill Zeke in on things at this end.''

"Yeah. I'd heard you managed to get yourself out of Mexico on your own. That was quite a miracle you pulled off, amigo. Why didn't you contact me and let me know you survived?"

"I wasn't in any shape to contact anyone there for a while.''

"What about later? You didn't contact me when you needed to get out of Mexico.''

"I know. I just headed north.''

"That was crazy, man. You know I would have done everything I could have to help." Zeke said with a frown.

"Yeah, I know. I still wasn't thinking very clearly.''

"That's quite a little memento you're carrying," Zeke said, motioning to the scar on Adam's forehead.

Adam absently rubbed the scar. "I've almost forgotten about it. It doesn't bother me much anymore.''

"You were damned lucky. You know that, don't you?"

"I know."

"Rob tells me the woman who nursed you back to health is your fiancée?"

"That's right."

"When am I going to meet this lady?"

"You know how it is, Zeke. We haven't been doing much socializing these days."

Zeke grinned. "Rob says she's quite good-looking."

"I think so."

"I know you. You're afraid I'm going to steal her away from you."

"Something like that."

"Seriously, I'd really like to meet her. Rob tells me she saw the man who tried to kill you."

Adam was finding himself more and more reluctant to continue the conversation. He didn't believe what Caitlin had told him, not for a minute. Zeke's questions and concerns were valid and directly connected with his work. But Adam's emotions had just gone through a wringer, and he wasn't up to much more at the moment.

"Yes, but she wasn't able to identify him from any of our mug shots."

"That's too bad. Is she in our office now? Maybe I'll go on back and introduce myself." Zeke stood up and stretched.

"No, I didn't bring her today. She was tired."

"So you left her sleeping in at the hotel, did you?"

"I think she was going to do some shopping."

"Where are you two staying?"

"At the Hilton."

"Good choice." He turned to Rob. "Well, guess I'll check my desk and see what's been happening. I'll talk to you guys later." He waved and walked out of the room.

Adam looked over at Rob. "Why did Zeke say he was up here? I didn't catch that."

"Oh, said he was checking out some leads. Seemed to be very interested in everything that had happened to you. He says you're one of his most valuable men down there. He was quite upset when he thought we'd lost you."

Damn Caitlin for planting doubts in Adam's mind. There was no reason to suspect Zeke, no reason in the world.

"How well do you know Zeke, Rob?"

"Hell, I don't know. As well as I know you, maybe. Zeke was here when I transferred in from Washington."

"When was that?"

"About eight years ago. Why?"

"I just wondered. He's been with the Agency a long time, then, hasn't he?"

"Fifteen years."

"And he's spent all his time in Mexico?"

"That's right. All but the first two years. Is there some point to all of this?"

"Isn't it unusual that he hasn't been promoted or transferred out?"

"He's turned down numerous promotions. Says he likes field work too much." Rob leaned forward. "What the hell is this all about?"

Adam sighed. He could either bury it right now or go with Caitlin's unsubstantiated report.

"Rob, only two people knew I had a meeting that night—Santiago and Zeke. I didn't make the meeting with Santiago's contact, as you know. Zeke was the only other person who knew I would be going out into the mountains."

"What are you saying?"

"I'm not sure. All I know is that I would swear I was not followed that night. Whoever came up behind me was waiting on some side road. Someone who knew where I would be going."

The two men sat across from each other. They both knew what the other was thinking. Their salaries were good but couldn't begin to compare with the kind of money generated by the rapidly expanding drug business.

If Zeke Taylor had succumbed, he wouldn't be the first agent who had been lured into switching allegiance. He wouldn't be the last.

But if he were straight, how could Adam ever face him again if he pointed the finger at him without any proof whatsoever? He didn't know what to do.

"I'm not telling you you're wrong, Adam," Rob said slowly, rubbing his chin thoughtfully. "But Zeke's the one who pulled this one out of the fire for us. He made the contact you intended to make, got the information and nailed Santiago."

"Yeah, I know. I've spent quite a lot of time thinking about that. However, just for the sake of argument, let's suppose that Zeke *is* involved—up to his eyeballs.... If that's the case, he would already have that information. He wouldn't have needed to get it from someone else."

"Suppose the information I was to get that night was something else entirely. Say...something about Zeke. Isn't it interesting that the informant turned up dead, right after Zeke saw him?"

"You're saying Zeke killed him?"

"I don't know what I'm saying. I'm just thinking out loud."

The men sat there in silence for an extended period of time—men who were trained to do mental gymnastics with any kind of information handed to them. Each of them knew better than to ignore the flimsiest of supposition. Sometimes the most unorthodox information led to the most revealing conclusions.

Eventually Rob sat back in his chair and sighed. He looked tired...almost defeated. There was nothing worse than a traitor in an organization. He'd been around too long not to know that they existed. But he never enjoyed having to face it.

"I could do some investigating if you think it's called for," Rob finally said. "Check on his bank accounts, that sort of thing. He couldn't hide that much extra income, although since he lives down in Mexico, we haven't kept tabs like we could if he were here."

"I don't know what to say, Rob. I really don't. I just have this sick feeling in the pit of my stomach. And I can't help but think about Caitlin's predicament if Zeke had anything to do with what happened to me."

"What do you mean?"

"She can identify the driver. And we have filled Zeke in on everything. If we can find the driver, and he can point the finger at Zeke—"

"That's assuming that the driver is working for Zeke."

"Yeah."

"And that's what you think."

"I don't know what I think."

"Well, dammit, that's what you're saying. Or did you watch too much television last night and dream up this whole scenario?" Rob hated to think where an investigation like this would end, but now that it had surfaced, he couldn't ignore it.

"I just think we need to look at the fact that no one else knew where I was going, that's all. Is that enough to start watching what Zeke is up to? Do we really know what leads he's following up here? Is it possible I'm one of his leads? And that now we've told him about Caitlin, he'll try to find out how much of a threat she is to him?"

Rob picked up the phone and pushed the intercom button. "Would you tell Zeke I'd like to see him?"

Adam glanced up in alarm. Surely he wasn't going to tell him what they were talking about. Not yet. They had no proof. They had nothing. And if Caitlin was right, they'd be giving him all the warning he needed to cover his tracks.

"Oh?" Rob said. "When did he leave?" He frowned at Adam. "I see. No, no problem." He hung up the phone, his frown growing.

"He's gone?"

"Yeah, said he had some things he wanted to do and probably wouldn't be back today."

"Which could be perfectly in line with his job."

"Yeah."

They both sat there for a few moments.

"Where's Caitlin?" Rob finally asked.

"I'm not sure. We had words earlier, and like an idiot I stormed out. I'm not particularly proud of my behavior."

"Don't be too hard on yourself, Adam. You've had a rough few months. We all get a little touchy when somebody's trying to kill us."

"Particularly if it happens to be a friend."

Rob stood up. "Why don't you get back to the hotel and make up with your fiancée? I'd feel a hell of a lot better if you didn't let her out of your sight for a few days, at least until I've had some things checked out." He looked over at the window for a moment, then his gaze returned to Adam. "We need to follow up on this one. I think your concerns are valid, but I hope you're wrong. Something like this is like a cancer in an organization. Once you open it up, you don't know how far it has spread or how fatal the disease." Sitting back down, he waved his hand toward the door.

"Go play besotted fiancé. I've got work to do."

Adam nodded and left the room. He agreed with Rob. He hoped they were wrong about Zeke. But if they weren't...if they weren't? Then Caitlin had given them information that they wouldn't have received from anywhere else. Zeke hadn't made any mistakes, so he thought he was safe.

However, he might feel that both Adam and Caitlin were expendable. Adam found himself walking faster. He needed to get back to the hotel, back to Caitlin.

He had to let her know how much he loved her.

Ten

By the time she heard the announcement that her flight was canceled, Caitlin felt numb, which she considered a blessing. All she wanted to do was to get back to her home and away from the mass of confusion that swirled around her. The announcement put an end to her plans of trying to get back that day.

She couldn't get Adam out of her mind. She still felt his pain and confusion, but she also felt his guilt over his behavior toward her. However, she wasn't ready to face him again. Too many things had been said, too many emotions had been bared. Someday, maybe, she would be able to sit down and discuss with him the fact that they could not have a relationship, but only after she gained some control over her emotions.

When would that be? she wondered. Well, maybe in another five years or so. Could she ever be unemotional where Adam was concerned, particularly if she ever saw him again? Caitlin seriously doubted it.

"Excuse me," she said to the harried airline official behind the counter.

"Yes, ma'am?"

"When is your next flight to Monterrey?"

"Tomorrow afternoon at 3:30."

"You don't have any other flights out today?"

"No, ma'am."

"Does any other airline fly to Monterrey?"

"Not from this airport."

"I see."

"I'm sorry, ma'am. There were problems with the engine of the plane scheduled for this flight, and the plane had to be grounded. We're doing the best we can."

"I'm sure you are," she murmured. "Thank you."

Now what was she to do?

She wished she knew.

Adam felt a distinct sinking sensation in his stomach when he returned to the room and found Caitlin gone. Of course, she could be out shopping, or sightseeing, but somehow he knew better. When he saw that her suitcase was gone, his worst fears were confirmed.

She'd left. And why not, after all the accusations he'd hurled at her? She had more intelligence than to sit around and wait for his next attack.

Adam called the front desk, knowing there was only a slim chance that someone had seen her leave. But he had to try. He had to do something before he faced the fact that Caitlin was gone.

"Can you tell me when my wife left the hotel?" He wasn't about to get into their marital situation with the desk clerk.

"No, sir, I'm afraid not. I came on at three today. Her key was already here."

Great. She left before three. And she took her luggage, which meant she had no intention of returning. Where would she go?

There was only one place Caitlin would go, her safe retreat from the world. He called the airport.

"What airlines fly to Monterrey?"

When he was given the name of the airline, he called their number, but there was no answer. He glanced at his watch. It was almost seven. What did no answer mean? Had they gone out of business? Gone bankrupt? Or did the pilot answer the phone when the plane was on the ground?

Oh, Caitlin, love, where are you? Do you have any idea how sorry I am for upsetting you? Do you know how much I love you? I've got this damnable temper, but I didn't mean to take it out on you. Please don't run. Please stay here and help me work this out. It's our problem and we need to solve it together.

He paced the floor, trying to decide what to do. Did he go out and walk the streets, go looking for her? And if so, where?

Adam decided to call Rob at home.

"Hello, Sara," he said, when Rob's wife answered. "This is Adam St. Clair. Rob around, by chance?"

He waited impatiently while he heard Sara call Rob to the phone.

"Yes, Adam? Anything new happening?"

"Caitlin's gone."

"What do you mean, gone?"

"I mean that she and her luggage are no longer in the room."

Adam listened patiently while Rob made a few choice comments, none of which were printable.

"My sentiments exactly," Adam added quietly when Rob paused for breath.

"That must have been one hell of a fight you had," Rob finally said. "Where do you think she's gone?"

"Back to her home."

"In Mexico?"

"Yeah."

"Well, that's just great, isn't it? If what we think is true, she's going to be a sitting duck down there."

"Maybe, except no one knows where she lives. That's why I wasn't found earlier."

"So you think maybe she's just as safe there as here?"

"I don't know what to think at this point. All I know is I have royally messed up this relationship, and I don't know where I'm going or what to do."

"Take it easy, old man. If what you suspect is true, your brilliant deductions may have cracked this drug ring wide open."

"They weren't my deductions, Rob. That's what all of this is about."

"What are you talking about?"

"The fight I had with Caitlin. She's psychic, clairvoyant, whatever the hell you call it. She picked up on the man, gave me his motivation, his thoughts and ideas, the whole thing, and I blew up at her."

Stunned silence greeted him for a moment. In a tentative tone, Rob asked, "You mean Caitlin's one of those people who gazes into a crystal ball and tells your future?''

''Not quite that dramatic, but along those lines, yes.''

''But you didn't believe her about our man.''

''Not at first, no.''

''What made you change your mind?''

''I'm not sure. I probably wouldn't have if he hadn't been in the office and I had an opportunity to be with him. Once she planted the idea in my head, it seemed to wipe away all my preconceived ideas of him. I had always seen him through the eyes of friendship. Today I watched him as I would watch any other possible suspect, and I picked up on things I wouldn't have noticed before.''

''Such as?''

''Mannerisms, body language, eye contact. That warm, friendly greeting I got looked great, and I probably would never have questioned it, but his eyes were cold, Rob. He was studying me, trying to figure out what I knew, if anything. I could almost feel it.''

''Maybe you're psychic, too,'' Rob said with a chuckle.

''You know as well as I do that our intuitive abilities get overworked in this business.''

''I know.''

''Well, mine kicked into overdrive during that session, Rob. By the time he left, I wasn't nearly so certain that Caitlin hadn't hit on something.''

''You've got a lot to be thankful for in that woman, you know.''

"I know. I've just got to find her and convince her that although I'm a complete clod I love her to distraction."

"I just wish we had something concrete to hang on him," Rob pointed out. "I made some phone calls down into the Interior right after you left. I skipped over all our standard means of communication and went to Mexico City. At the moment we don't dare trust any of our usual pipelines. I explained the urgency. We should be hearing something soon."

"Thanks, Rob. I appreciate your going through all of this."

"Well, I won't pretend that I don't hope you two are proved wrong."

"I feel the same way."

"Call me as soon as you hear something from Caitlin."

"If...that's the operative word."

"This is just temporary for you two—any fool could tell that. There's an energy field around the two of you that almost lights up, it's so strong. And I don't have to be able to predict the future to know you'll work this thing out."

"I appreciate the vote of confidence. I'll talk to you later."

Adam hung up the phone, feeling somewhat better. Rob was right. There was no way he was going to allow Caitlin to disappear from his life. At the moment his greatest concern was to protect her. If what he suspected was true, bringing her to San Antonio had increased the danger to her considerably.

Sighing, he dropped into the chair in front of the window and gazed out at the night.

* * *

Caitlin had lost track of time. She felt as though she'd spent days at the airport, but when she caught a taxi back downtown, she realized she'd been gone for only a few hours.

At least sitting there waiting for a plane that never took off had given her some time to think. Her thoughts hadn't been particularly pleasant. She'd had to face that she was a coward, something that she had suspected but had oftentimes tried to deny.

She was running away. Just as she had run away before. When was she going to stop running and confront her fears?

She loved Adam. She knew that he loved her. Didn't she have enough faith in them to believe that whatever their problems they could work them out?

Adam's love seemed to surge around her in heavy waves as though he were sending messages to her. By the time she got into the taxi, Caitlin knew that she had to return to the hotel and face Adam.

Perhaps that plane hadn't taken off for a reason. She'd been given another chance to rethink her position. Caitlin didn't believe in coincidences. As much as she dreaded facing him again, she knew that she needed to see Adam.

There were a great many cars and taxis in front of the Hilton, and she suggested the driver of her taxi let her out nearby. After she paid him, she grabbed her bag and started down the street toward the main entrance.

A sense of unease settled over her, and she paused. Something was wrong. Without analyzing her feeling, Caitlin knew that she needed to bypass the lobby

area. She went into a boutique that had entrances on
both the street and inside the hotel. Watching the
hallway, she left the boutique and quietly went toward the lobby.

What was wrong?

The lobby, like the parking area, was filled with a
milling group of people, conventioneers from the look
of it. She felt no threat from any of them.

Then her mind's eye clearly focused on a man who
was across the lobby, talking to a bellhop—a man with
dark hair and eyes and a closely-trimmed beard.

Zeke Taylor.

She had no idea what he was doing in San Antonio
but knew without a doubt that he was looking for her.
Hastily stepping back, she glanced around and spotted the stairway that led upstairs. After climbing to the
next floor, Caitlin got on the elevator and rode to the
floor where she and Adam had spent the night before.

When she started down the hallway, Caitlin realized that she hadn't stopped for her key. She could
only pray that Adam was in the room. Pausing for a
moment, she took a deep breath and exhaled, forcing
herself to relax. She tapped lightly on the door and
waited, forcing herself not to hold her breath.

Adam heard a soft tap on the door, and he sprang
from his chair. Few people knew he was there. Zeke
was one of them. He had his pistol in his hand when
he asked quietly from the other side of the door,
"Who is it?"

"Caitlin."

Adam threw open the door, grabbed her and hauled
her into his arms. Kicking the door closed behind her,

he held her tightly against him, his forgotten gun pressed against her back.

"Oh, God, Caitlin. I've been so worried. Where the hell have you been? I've been about out of my mind!"

Not giving her a chance to answer him, he began to kiss her, then he seemed to remember that he still held his pistol in his hand, and he paused, looking down at her.

"Do you have any idea how much I love you, lady?" he asked, his voice so gruff she could barely understand him.

"I love you, too, Adam. And I don't blame you for your doubts. I'm just so afraid at the moment."

He'd laid the gun down by the bed and gathered her in his arms once again. "Don't be. Everything's going to work out all right. You'll see. Everything's going to be fine."

"Adam?"

"Hmmm?"

"I know how you feel about Zeke and all. I just think you should know he's in San Antonio."

"Yes, I know. I saw him—" He looked down at her again. "How did you know? Did you pick up something—"

"He's downstairs in the lobby."

"Here?"

"Yes."

He immediately dropped his arms from around her and walked away.

"I know he's your friend, and I understand how you feel, but I'm afraid of him."

"Yeah, well, I can understand that."

"Do you think he's coming up here?"

"There's a strong possibility. I told him where we were staying, and he said he'd like to meet you."

She felt a shiver run over her spine.

"Don't worry; I have no intention of letting him see you. Your best protection from him at the moment is that he doesn't know what you look like."

There was a knock at the door, and they stared at each other. Adam put a finger to his lips, then asked, "Who is it?"

"Zeke."

Adam glanced around, saw Caitlin's bag and picked it up. In three strides he'd placed it in the bathroom, behind the door, motioned for her to get into the shower, then went back to the door and opened it.

"Well, hello, Zeke. I didn't expect to see you. Come on in."

Zeke wore the same clothes he'd had on earlier. He walked in, glanced around the room, then went over by the windows and sat down.

"Where's your fiancée?"

"Good question."

"What do you mean?"

"I guess I must have made her madder than I thought this morning. When I came back, she was gone, bag and baggage."

Zeke laughed. "Some ladies' man you are, St. Clair. Thought I'd trained you better than to let 'em get away from you like that."

Adam shrugged and sat down across from him. "So what are you up to?"

"Oh, nothing much. Thought I'd stop by and take you guys out for a drink, meet your lady love, that sort of thing."

"Guess you're out of luck, then."

"Where do you suppose she went?"

"Who knows? Probably back to the mountains."

"You never did tell me where you were for all that time. Those mountains are pretty vast."

"To be honest, I couldn't tell you, myself."

"Well, the important thing is that you survived."

"Thanks to Caitlin."

"Yes. Thanks to Caitlin." He looked around the room again. "So. How about you and me going for that drink? It beats sitting around a hotel room and feeling sorry for yourself."

"I'm sure it does, but I don't think I'm up to it tonight. I still get tired easily, and after the past couple of days, I'm pretty beat."

Zeke stood up. "Sure, I understand. I guess I'll see you at the office tomorrow."

"When are you going back to Mexico?"

"I'm not sure, exactly. My plans are still up in the air. What about you?"

"I've been thinking about asking for a leave of absence. There's work that needs to be done around the ranch, and Dane's had his hands full."

"You thinking about giving up your work for the Agency?"

"The thought has crossed my mind more than once these past few months."

"It's a tough business."

"I know. I don't know how you've managed to stay with it so long."

"Oh, it gets in your blood after a while. You get so you can't live without the excitement, that extra boost of adrenaline that comes in from time to time."

"Better you than me." Adam walked him to the
door. "I'll see you tomorrow."

Zeke gave a casual wave of his hand and walked out.
Adam closed the door, put the night latch on and listened at the door until he heard the elevator arrive.
Once he heard the clang of the elevator doors closing,
he turned around and found Caitlin standing in the
doorway to the bathroom.

"You know about him, don't you?" she said softly.

His eyes met hers. "I do now." Adam walked over
to her and began to unbutton her blouse.

"What are you doing?"

"Getting ready for bed."

"Adam, we need to talk."

"I know. I find I can talk better horizontal."

"I'm sorry for running out that way—" Her words
died away as she felt his lips pressed along her neck.

"I'm sorry for being a complete fool when you were
trying to save both of us," he replied, peeling away her
blouse and dropping it to the floor.

"Adam—"

He unfastened her skirt and let it fall to the floor,
then pushed her remaining undergarments down.
Picking her up, he put her on the bed, where the covers had been turned back by room service.

"Adam, I know how you must feel—"

"Good," he muttered, hurriedly stripping out of his
clothes, "then I don't have to explain my intentions."

"No, I mean about Zeke and . . . everything . . . Oh,
Adam."

His mouth had found her breast, and he tenderly
touched his tongue to the peak, his hand gently
squeezing the other one.

"I love you, Caitlin," he murmured.

Caitlin was having trouble concentrating on his words. His mouth and hands were using a language all their own, one that caused her body to react in ways that she had no control over.

"Oh, Adam, I love you, too."

"Don't give up on me yet, love. Give me some time to get used to all of your talents and abilities, okay?" His mouth had touched her intimately, and she could no longer think. She could only feel. Oh, what he did to her, this man. How could she have possibly thought she could leave him? He was too much a part of her. He always would be.

By the time he raised himself above her, Caitlin felt reduced to a mass of sensations, knowing that Adam was the only man in all the world who could fulfill her. She silently prayed that she could be all that he wanted and needed in return.

His possession of her was more than physical. It was as though their very spirits were entwined, and they became lost in the mutual sharing.

Whatever happened, they would face it together. Whatever dangers there were, they would share. Each had something to teach the other—about life, about a heightened awareness, about love.

They had a whole lifetime in which to learn.

Adam and Caitlin fell asleep in each other's arms. The traumas of the day had exhausted them both. Even in sleep they clung to each other, as though aware of how close they had come to losing what they had.

The phone rang several times before Adam was awake enough to answer it. "H'lo?"

"Good news," Rob McFarlane said cryptically.

Adam blinked a couple of times, trying to get awake. He reached over and turned on the bedside light and pushed himself up on the pillow.

"That right?"

"My inquiry detonated a powder keg down south. Seems they've been working on something similar, but going through different sources. The evidence has been mounting up, but they couldn't put a name or face to it. Until tonight. As soon as I furnished that, everything clicked and fell into place. We've got him, Adam. Got him cold."

"Why can't I feel better about that?"

"He almost succeeded in killing you, Adam."

Adam glanced at Caitlin lying next to him, asleep. Her tousled hair fell across her shoulders, and her hand rested under her cheek. For the first time he realized she wasn't wearing his ring.

He suddenly remembered that she had wanted to talk. He hadn't given her much of a chance to make any explanations.

She'd responded to him, had admitted that she loved him, but she'd taken off his ring. Why had he thought that by taking her to bed he had solved the rift between them?

"Adam? Did you go back to sleep?" Rob's voice sounded amused.

"No, I'm not asleep. But I haven't been thinking very clearly, either."

"That's understandable. It's close to three-thirty in the morning. I'm sorry to wake you up, but I thought you'd want to know."

"When are you going to make the arrest?"

"In the morning. There's some paperwork to get done. And I've got to make sure he can't get out on bail. If he does, we'll never see him again. If he were to get across the border, he'd be gone."

"Are you going to need me for anything?"

"No. You've done enough. You deserve some time off."

"Thanks. I need it."

"I expect a wedding invitation, you know."

"You'll get one," he replied. *If there's going to be a wedding,* he added silently.

Adam reached over and turned off the light after hanging up the phone, but he continued to lie there, propped up on his pillow. He had a lot to think about. And the biggest selling job he'd ever faced waited for him when Caitlin woke up. He wanted to be ready for it.

Eventually he dozed, sleeping fitfully, his dreams jumbled, but Adam was so aware of Caitlin that he knew the moment she woke up the next morning.

He opened his eyes and looked at her. She was on her side, close enough that he could feel the warmth of her body.

"Good morning," he said, trying to read her expression.

She smiled. "Did I hear the phone ring last night, or was I dreaming?"

"It rang. Rob called to say they had the necessary evidence to pick up Zeke."

"Oh." She propped herself up on her elbow and looked at him. "I know how badly you must feel."

There were degrees of feeling badly, he thought wryly. Losing a friend was tough. Losing your love was a hell of a lot tougher.

She was so endearing. He wished he knew what she was thinking at that moment. He almost envied her the ability to look into another person's head.

"Looks like the case is wrapped up," he offered. "So there's no reason to stay here."

She sat up and stretched. "I know that's a load off your mind, even though it didn't end as you would have hoped. Now you can put all of the past few months behind you and get on with your life." Turning around and looking at him, still stretched out beside her, she asked, "Did you mean what you said to Zeke last night? About getting out of the business?"

"I've given it some thought. Why?"

"I just wondered."

"So what do you want to do now?" Why did his heart rate seem to pick up just because he'd finally put the key question to her?

"Go back to the cabin, I suppose."

Well. He had his answer. Funny that he'd thought all of his fears were behind him. What could he say to that? He couldn't hold her captive on the ranch. She was independent, determined—very determined—stubborn, even. Having previously agreed to marry him didn't lock her into anything. That's what engagements were for, after all. They were a trial period, a testing. And he had flunked the test.

"Do you want me to drive you back?" He was proud of his voice. He sounded carefully neutral, as though his insides weren't churning.

Caitlin paused from sliding out of bed and looked at him, really looked at him. The lighthearted, teasing man she had just begun to know was gone. In his place was the quiet stranger she had nursed back to health.

What was wrong? And why did he ask such a question?

"Don't you want to take me back?"

His eyes looked wintry as they met her puzzled gaze. "Shall I be polite or honest?"

"Okay, so you don't want to make another trip down there. I can understand that." Caitlin stood up and pulled on her robe. "I can fly down there from here, I suppose. But how do you suggest I get everything moved from down there to the ranch?"

Her words seemed to shoot a charge of energy through him, and he sat up straight. "The ranch? You're moving to the ranch?"

Caitlin looked at him, worried about his mental condition. She knew he'd been under a tremendous strain for some time. Maybe this latest news had been too much for him. She walked around to his side of the bed and sat down. Taking his hand, she lovingly stroked it between her fingers, lifting it so that she could kiss his knuckles.

"Adam. Most new marriages are begun under a considerable strain. I'm sure ours won't be an exception." She held his palm against her cheek, loving the feel of its work-roughened surface. "I think it only fair that we make the transition between our single and married states as painless as possible. We really need to be together to make it work.''

He slid his hand behind her neck and pulled her mouth over to his. When they were only inches apart, Adam muttered between clenched teeth, ''Is that your humorous way of trying to tell me that you intend to marry me, after all?''

She blinked her eyes. ''What do you mean, after all?''

His mouth clamped tightly to hers in a hard, possessive kiss that left no doubt in her mind that he was perturbed about something. However, it also made it quite clear that he wanted her very badly. By the time he eased the pressure, Caitlin had totally forgotten what they'd been talking about.

Adam hadn't. ''Where is your ring?''

She opened her eyes, surprised at his steely tone of voice.

''My ring? Oh! I forgot.'' Scrambling off the bed, Caitlin hurried over to Adam's suitcase and delved into it. Picking up the envelope she'd left there, she ripped it open and took the ring out. Very carefully she slipped it on her finger and returned to the bed. ''There.'' She smiled at him, a very warm, loving smile.

''Why did you take it off?''

''You know why. I thought our argument proved how unsuited we were and that it proved how right I'd been all along not to get involved with anyone.''

He glanced down at the diamond glittering on her hand.

''And now?''

"Now I know that you'll hate it when I know what you're thinking, but it's okay, because we both know the only thing that really matters is that we love each other. That's what counts."

He pulled her down on top of him. "You are a very wise lady, Caitlin Moran. I think you must be a witch."

She chuckled. "That's what the villagers used to call me. Of course they know better now."

"Oh, do they?"

"I'm really very ordinary."

"Um-hm." He began to nibble on her ear. "Caitlin?"

"Yes, love."

"Would you please check your crystal ball and see if there's any reason we have to hurry down to Mexico today?"

"I can't think of any. Can you?"

"No, I can't. I was thinking that maybe we'd want to spend some time today planning our honeymoon."

"You mean this isn't it?"

He rolled over, pulling her down beside him, and began to untie her robe. "No, ma'am. This has been just a preview."

Caitlin ran her hands along his back and shoulders and smiled. "Then I can hardly wait for the main event."

* * * * *

Silhouette Desire

Available
August 1987

ONE TOUGH HOMBRE

Visit with characters introduced
in the acclaimed Desire trilogy
by Joan Hohl!

The *Hombre* is back!
J. B. Barnet—first introduced in *Texas Gold*—
has returned and make no mistake,
J.B. *is* one tough hombre . . . but
Nicole Vanzant finds the gentle,
tender side of the former
Texas Ranger.

Don't miss *One Tough Hombre*—
J.B. and Nicole's story.
And coming soon from Desire is
Falcon's Flight—the story of Flint Falcon
and Leslie Fairfield.

D372-1R

Silhouette Desire

COMING NEXT MONTH

#373 INTRUSIVE MAN—Lass Small
How could Hannah Calhoun continue to run her boardinghouse with any semblance of sanity when all her paying guests were pushing her into the all-too-willing arms of Officer Maxwell Simmons?

#374 HEART'S DELIGHT—Ashley Summers
Cabe McLain was resigned to a life of single parenthood—but that was before Laura Richards showed him that her childhood friendship had ripened into a woman's love.

#375 A GIFT OF LOVE—Sherryl Woods
Meg Blake had learned early on that most problems were best dealt with alone. Matt Flanagan was the one to show her otherwise—teaching her firsthand the power of love.

#376 SOMETHING IN COMMON—Leslie Davis Guccione
Confirmed bachelor Kevin Branigan, the "cranberry baron" from STILL WATERS (Desire #353), met Erin O'Connor—and more than met his match!

#377 MEET ME AT MIDNIGHT—Christine Flynn
Security agent Matt Killian did things by-the-book. He had no intention of having an unpredictable—and all too attractive—Eden Michaels on his team. But soon Matt found himself throwing caution to the winds.

#378 THE PRIMROSE PATH—Joyce Thies
It took an outrageous scheme from their respective grandparents to find the adventurous hearts beneath banker Clay Chancelor's and CPA Carla Valentine's staid exteriors. Neither imagined that the prize at the end of the chase was love.

AVAILABLE NOW:

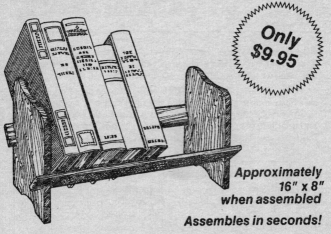

09.50